Praise for David

Swimmin

"I love books that can destroy their own labels…David-Matthew Barnes' marvelous *Swimming to Chicago* will doubtless be put on the YA shelf…a well-told tale…that will engross readers of all ages…riveting…"—Jerry Wheeler, *Out in Print*

"I found myself unable to put it down…"—Sara Power, *Books Your Kids Will Love*

"This was a heartbreaking story…I enjoyed the book. It made me think once again about how we need to fight for acceptance…this book highlighted the need to stop bullying and the fears gay high school students have when deciding whether or not to reveal their sexuality."—*Lilly Road*

"Like many teenagers, Alex just wants to belong and to be truly liked…*Swimming to Chicago* provides twists, shock and escape…"—Amy Steele, *Entertainment Realm*

Mesmerized

"Barnes' young adult novel about two boys suddenly, deeply in love has a fairy-tale tone, but it will strike all the right notes for YA readers as the boys dance into the hearts of The Showdown audience."—Richard Labonté, *BookMarks*

"There is a wonderful resounding theme: sometimes you have to be brave enough to love and forgive. You won't grasp these words completely unless you read this entire heartrending story…"— *QMO (Queer Magazine Online)*

"…a timely work that will resonate with readers for its portrayal of society's perception of the GLBT community…" —*Out & About*

Soliloquy titles by the Author

Mesmerized

Swimming to Chicago

Wonderland

WONDERLAND

by

David-Matthew Barnes

A Division of Bold Strokes Books

2013

CREDITS
EDITORS: GREG HERREN AND STACIA SEAMAN
PRODUCTION DESIGN: STACIA SEAMAN
COVER DESIGN BY SHERI (GRAPHICARTIST2020@HOTMAIL.COM)

Acknowledgments

Wonderland could not have happened without Cindy Cresap, Greg Herren, Len Barot, Sheri, and Stacia Seaman.

For their never-ending support and words of encouragement, I offer my deepest gratitude to:

Albert Magaña, Andrea Patten, Bethany Hidden-Cauley, Cathy Moreno, Cyndi Lopez, Donna Cummings, Elizabeth Warren, Frankie Hernandez, Heather Brant, January Cummings, Jessica Moreno, Joyce Luzader, Keshia Whitmore-Govers, Kimberly Greenberg, Linda Wread-Barnes, Maire Gardner, Marisa Villegas, Michelle Boman Harris, Mindy Morgan, Nance Haxton, Nick A. Moreno, Nita Manley, Patricia Abbott-Dinsmore, Rena Mason, Robyn Colburn, Sabra Rahel, Sal Meza, Selena Ambush, Stacy Scranton, Stefani Deoul, Stephanie Gomez, Susan Madden, Tara Henry, Therease Logan, Trish DeBaun, Todd Wylie, and Vanessa Menendez.

To my parents, Samuel Barnes, Jr. and Nancy Nickle, and my brothers Jamin, Jason, Andy, and Jaren, for allowing me to be the writer in the family.

To my students, for teaching me more on a daily basis than I could ever dream of teaching them.

To the loving memory of my grandmother, Dorothy Helen Nickle, for my childhood of soap operas and tea parties.

To Edward C. Ortiz, for the wonderful life and love we share.

To the beautiful people I have lost who still resonate in every word I write: Caitlin Quinn, Dorothy Helen Nickle, Judy Ron, Malena Hamilton, Marianne Psota, and Norman Michael Parent.

To God, for everything.

For my mother, Nancy Anne Nickle,
for teaching me to choose love.
And for always encouraging us to dance
around the living room.

CHAPTER ONE

D o you believe in magic?" the mustached dark-haired man onstage asked me. Wearing a tuxedo shirt, wrinkled dark slacks, a black cape lined with crushed red velvet, and shiny black shoes, he was holding a top hat in one hand and a glittery-tipped wand in the other. Standing beneath the glare of a harsh spotlight, he was sweating and waiting for my answer from where I was sitting in the dark theater on a wooden folding chair.

I couldn't stop thinking about how hilarious his crooked toupée looked.

And the fact I was related to him.

I glanced around at my new surroundings and decided the best answer to give was simply "Yes."

He squinted and shielded his eyes with the edge of his hand from the light, and searched for me in the back row. "Are you comfortable working with animals?"

I thought of my younger brother and answered, "I have some experience in that area."

The theater was tiny and old. The walls were painted sea blue. The thick, red stage curtains were covered with gold and silver metallic stars. The temperature was cool and comfortable. I felt safe there, calm.

Like I was in another world where something really fun and exciting was about to happen.

"One last question," he said, "and it's the most important one."

I sat up. My chair creaked. "Ask me anything."

Uncle Fred curled his hands into fists and placed them on his hips. He looked like a superhero, waiting for a reason to fly off somewhere to fight crime. "Can you keep a secret?" he asked.

Not according to my best friend Samantha, I thought. She'd said I had the biggest mouth in Chicago. Since I now lived more than a thousand miles away from her and everything I'd ever known in a place called Avalon Cove, I wondered if I'd ever see her again. "Of course I can," I said, knowing it was a lie.

"Great," he said. "You start tomorrow, Destiny."

"Thanks, Uncle Fred."

He waved a finger at me. "You can call me Uncle Fred at home. Here, I'm Sir Frederic the Great," he informed me.

I heard a man's voice from behind me. "Will Sir Frederic the Great like peas or green beans with his meatloaf tonight?" shouted my other uncle from the closet-sized light and sound booth in the back of the theater. His name was Clark. He'd been a part of our family for as long as I could remember. He was younger than Uncle Fred by at least a decade. Clark wasn't really my uncle—at least not biologically. He was fortunate enough to be born into a more normal family than mine. I couldn't figure out how he ended up falling in love with my crazy Uncle Fred. But one thing for sure was they were perfect for each other.

It was only my first day in Avalon Cove. Already I knew my mother had made the right choice. Uncle Fred and Clark were now my legal guardians. I'd be living with them for the next two and a half years until I turned eighteen.

"Peas or green beans?" Uncle Fred repeated. "Do you

have to ask? My answer is always carrots." With that, he made an adorable white rabbit pop out of his top hat.

"Awwwww," I heard myself say.

Clark was now standing next to my chair. He always smelled good, like sweet soap. He was skinny, sexy, and had great hair. "I need to finish up some paperwork and feed Carrots her dinner," he said. "If I show you how, would you mind watching the gift shop for me?"

"Sure." I stood. "No prob."

We left Uncle Fred and Carrots onstage. I followed Clark through the double doors leading out to the sunlit lobby. I blinked as my eyes adjusted. Standing there, I felt like a fish in a bowl. We were facing a curved wall of floor-to-ceiling windows. I could see the sidewalk in front of the theater through them, and an adorable café across the street. In the not-so-far distance to my left was the Atlantic shore.

When I'd arrived by cab less than an hour ago, I'd stood in front of the Magic Mansion, clutching the handles of my suitcases and staring at the odd-shaped circular building. From the outside it looked like a spaceship that had crash-landed a few blocks away from the beach. That's exactly how I felt: I was an alien just arrived from another planet called Chicago. There, my life had been "L" trains and selling corndogs and cotton candy part-time at Navy Pier. In Avalon Cove, it would be working at the Magic Mansion and living with my gay uncles. I was secretly hoping for beach parties and seaside make-out sessions with a hot boy—or maybe two. I'd been seriously deprived in the love department since last February, when a loser named Steve broke up with me on Valentine's Day by way of a candygram he sent to my Life Science class.

I mean, *who* does that?

"This," Clark said with a dramatic wave of his hand, "is our gift shop."

In the far corner of the lobby was a makeshift magic gift shop, consisting of a cluttered display case, a cash register that had to be a hundred years old at least, and five wooden shelves and two spinning racks crammed with every magic show souvenir imaginable.

Including some tacky do-it-yourself magic tricks.

"Glamorous, isn't it?" he asked.

I smiled and tucked a few strands of hair behind my ear. "Chicago's got nothing on this place."

"We rarely get a customer unless we have a show scheduled," he explained. "So I doubt anyone will come in, especially on a Wednesday afternoon. Have you worked a cash register before?"

"Once. I helped my best friend Samantha out. Her mom owns a natural food store." I stared at the archaic beast of a register. It was an antique. "How old is that thing?"

"It belonged to your grandfather," Clark said with a dimpled smile. "He was also a magician."

"Yeah," I said. "My mom used to tell me stories about him. And growing up in this place. She worked here, too."

"Your uncle insisted that everything stay the same," Clark explained. "Just as your grandfather left it when he died."

"If he was also a magician, couldn't he have made a new cash register appear?" I joked. "One that would be easier for his future granddaughter to use?"

"It's pretty simple," Clark said. "I can show you, if you want."

"Please do," I said. "Otherwise I might have to give everything away for free."

Clark gestured for me to join him behind the counter.

"I don't know much about this side of my family," I explained. "I remember meeting you once…when you and

Uncle Fred came to Chicago when I was seven…and then last week…at the funeral. You were so sweet to me that day. Thank you."

Clark locked eyes with me and placed a comforting hand on my shoulder. "We're very happy you're here, Destiny," he said. "I know we don't know each other very well, but we *are* family."

I swallowed and hoped I wouldn't cry. "There's just so much I never knew…about my grandfather and Uncle Fred… and the magic. What it was like for my mom when she was younger…living on this island."

Clark smiled. "You'll fall in love with Avalon Cove just like I have."

The black phone next to the register rang. The sound was loud and shrill and it made me jump. Clark grinned at me and picked up the heavy-looking receiver. "The Magic Mansion," he said. He looked at me and held the receiver up. "I think it's for you."

I gave him a look of surprise. "Me?" I said. "Who would call me?"

"I don't know," he said with a wink, "but it's a boy."

I took the phone from him and muttered, "It's probably my ridiculous brother telling me how much he loves life in California with Aunt Barbara."

"I have one of those, too," he said. "A ridiculous brother. Not an Aunt Barbara."

"Hello?" I said into the phone.

There was static and a crackling sound on the other end. "Hello?" I repeated.

"Destiny?" It was indeed a boy's voice. Soft and warm. Like an embrace through the phone. It was definitely *not* my brother.

"Yes?"

More static. More crackle. "I'm waiting for you," he said. "Come find me."

There was a click and the dial tone hummed in my ear. I hung up the phone. I tried to shake off the tiny tingle of adrenaline tiptoeing through my veins. There was something about the guy's voice on the phone…

"Who was it?" Clark asked.

"He didn't say. I'm sure it was just Ian being dumb and bored."

"You gotta love little brothers."

I then tried to focus on the complicated instructions Clark was sharing with me about the vintage cash register.

"It's solid brass, so it's worth a fortune," he said. "Or so I'm told."

I nodded. I smiled.

"Do you think you'll be okay on your own?" he asked, only a few moments later.

"Um…yeah…sure," I said, trying to convince us both. "Go do what you need to do. I'll be fine here."

"Great. Maybe I can convince Sir Frederic the Great to actually go home. He works too much." Clark opened one of the double doors of the theater entrance. He looked back. "I think you'll be really happy here," he said with a smile.

And even though I'd only been in the state of South Carolina for less than two hours, I believed him.

"I think so, too," I answered. "My mom knew this would be the best place for me."

Clark and I locked eyes. "She was a beautiful woman," he said.

I nodded and blinked back tears. "Yes, she was."

"You remind me of her," he said. "You're graceful, like she was."

Considering my mother had been a dance teacher, I took Clark's words as a compliment. He disappeared inside the theater. I wiped my eyes with the back of my hand, hoping the cheap mascara I was wearing hadn't turned into black puddles.

I stared at the monstrous buttons on the cash register and thought about my relatives who had lived and died before me. Some had worked exactly where I stood. The Magic Mansion had been in our family for generations. Yet until that afternoon, I'd never been there.

I knew Avalon Cove was a special place to my mother. After all, it's where she'd met my father the summer *she* was fifteen. They'd fallen in love, drifted apart, reconnected, got engaged, broke it off, reunited, eloped, had me and my ridiculous brother. Shortly after that, my father decided he'd be happier with someone else. My mother opened a dance studio in Chicago and never remarried. My father hooked up with a slutty flight attendant named Sandy. Their relationship—if you can call it that—lasted less than a year. I suspected my mom and dad were still in love right up until the end, in her hospital room when my father had to decide to turn off the machines keeping my mother alive.

For a moment, I tried to imagine what my mom had looked like standing behind the counter of the gift shop, leaning over the insane cash register. She was probably bored, flipping through a magazine, chewing gum and blowing bubbles. I pictured her practicing ballet positions with her feet, hoping to meet some cute guy she could flirt with for the last few weeks of summer. I wondered if she thought about leaving Avalon Cove while she spent summer after summer working in the Magic Mansion and day after day living in my grandfather's bizarre world of white rabbits and top hats. Did she want out? Or was this place truly home to her?

Maybe that's why you sent me here, Mom? So I could come back here for you?

I could feel someone watching me. I turned to the wall of windows. I was right. Friendly brown eyes were staring at me through the glass.

She was tall, beanpole-thin, and looked to be around the same age as me. I wondered if she was a ballerina. She certainly looked like one. Probably on her way to a class or a recital. I felt dumb for staring at her, but it was hard not to. She was so pretty, it was difficult to look away. Her dark hair was short and pushed out of her face with a thick yellow headband. Her catlike eyes locked with mine. And then she smiled at me. In that second, I felt like we'd been best friends for years even though she was a complete stranger.

She motioned for me to come outside and join her. I noticed her short fingernails were painted pastel purple. I shook my head, pointed to the register, and gestured for her to come in.

I could smell the salty sea breeze floating inside when she walked in, like a cloud of ocean air perfume. She moved to the counter, folded her arms across her chest, and said with a quick nod of her head, "You're new." Her voice had a tinge of toughness to it.

"I'm Destiny."

She repeated my name, making it sound exotic. "I already know who you are."

I gave her a look. "You do?"

"Yeah, I heard you were coming."

"Do you know my uncles?" I asked.

"Everybody does," she told me. "It's a small island."

"I just landed a couple of hours ago."

"From outer space?" She grinned.

I smiled. I liked her already. "No. From Chicago."

"Wow. Do you hate it here?"

"No…I like it. I mean, so far. I've never lived on an island before," I said.

"I was born here," she explained. "It used to be boring."

"It's not anymore?"

"No…now that you're finally here. I really hope you wanna be friends, Destiny. I don't have any."

"You don't have any friends?" I asked. *I hope that didn't sound bitchy.*

"No…that's not true," she said. "I have one friend. His name's Topher McGentry. I'm sure you'll meet him soon. Everyone else treats me like I'm toxic."

"You don't seem poisonous to me," I told her.

"Consider yourself warned. I'm a dork and not ashamed to admit it."

"Care to elaborate?" I asked.

"I'm one of three black girls in my high school," she said. "I like comic books and I love anime. I'm not into hip-hop. Or rap. Or Beyoncé. I'm a diehard vegan and I hate people who refuse to recycle. I don't hang out at parties and I refuse to go to school dances. Guys avoid me like the plague, which is perfectly fine with me, since I'm bi and I think girls are *way* hotter than boys. When I graduate in two years, I'm considering joining the Peace Corps. Or maybe starting an all-girl punk band. I can't decide. Maybe you can help me make up my mind."

I stared at her in awe, unsure of what to say.

She suddenly seemed really uncomfortable. "Should I go?" she asked. "I can leave. If you don't wanna be friends, I totally understand."

She turned toward the door. I reached out and tried to touch her arm but grabbed the short sleeve of her dark blue top instead. "No…I do. I definitely wanna be friends."

"Great," she said. "Then it's your turn to spill your guts."

"Okay…"

"Go," she instructed.

I took a quick breath before I spoke. "I've been here for a total of two hours. I'm from Chicago. My mom died almost two weeks ago. My uncles are now my legal guardians. I'm completely cool with them being gay. To me, people are people. I'm not bi, but my last boyfriend was a total jerk and broke up with me in a candygram on Valentine's Day. I wish my dad and I were closer, but he's too busy trying to hook up with girls who are half his age. My little brother Ian makes me crazy. I tried being a vegetarian for a week. I hated it and passed out. I've never read comic books. And I don't know what the Peace Corps is. But I used to dream about being in a band. Or having a beagle."

"Are you a swimmer?"

I shook my head "No. Why? Do I look I like one?"

She nodded. "Yeah, you do. Maybe it's the blond hair. And because you're tall…like me."

"You hate my hair?"

"Is it natural?"

"Yes."

"Yeah, I can tell."

"I usually don't wear it up in a ponytail," I explained. "It was hot on the plane."

"It's hot outside," she said. "The humidity here is a killer."

"Do people tell you that you look like Rihanna?" I asked.

"They do, and I usually forgive them for it," she said. "I'm not a fan."

"Me either," I lied.

She looked me in the eye. "Yes, you are," she decided.

"Girls like you always like her music. And girls like you always think I look like her, even though my style is completely different."

"What do you mean *girls like me*?" I asked.

"You know…the pretty but shy type. I bet you were really popular at your old school. In Chicago."

"Hardly," I said. Samantha and I usually kept to ourselves. There were a few kids we hung out with once in a while, but it was usually just the two of us.

"You will be here," she said. "Without even trying."

"What's your name?" I asked.

We both turned toward the theater's double doors as my uncles appeared, ready to lock up and go home. Uncle Fred had taken off his cape and unbuttoned the top button of his tuxedo shirt. Clark had keys in his hand and a burgundy windbreaker tossed over one shoulder. They looked like an odd couple: young, sexy Clark with his amazing cheekbones standing next to my toupée-wearing fortysomething strange uncle. I wondered what they saw in each other. What was the appeal?

It has to be true love.

"Hello, Tasha," my Uncle Fred said to my new friend. "It's good to see you again."

Her eyes lit up at the sight of Uncle Fred like he was a rock star. "Hello, Sir Frederic." I thought she was going to break into a full-blown curtsy or fall at his feet. "Do you mind if I show Destiny around the island for a while?"

He didn't give it much thought. He answered right away. "That would be all right. Just have her home by nine."

"She'll be in safe hands," Tasha promised.

"I'll save you a plate," Clark assured me. "You're welcome to join us, Tasha. I'm making meatloaf."

"Thanks for the invite, but I'm still a vegan," she explained.

"If you change your mind..." Clark said.

"Yeah," she said. "I probably will."

❖

"Don't be fooled by this place," Tasha cautioned. "It's pretty because of the ocean and the white sand, but there's nothing to do here, especially once the vacationers are gone."

So far, Avalon Cove seemed quiet, almost deserted. "Are they here now?" I asked, glancing around but seeing no one.

We were walking through a series of narrow, cobblestoned streets lined with ivy-covered boutiques, antique shops, French bistros, pubs, and a bakery. Between them, or stacked above, were shuttered apartments, complete with wrought-iron terraces and brightly colored flowerboxes.

This is what Europe must be like. Maybe I can pretend I don't live in Avalon Cove, South Carolina. I live in a little village, just outside of Paris. In fact, I can see the Eiffel Tower in the distance where my hot French lover is waiting for me. No. Wait. That's not the Eiffel Tower, it's a palm tree. They don't have palm trees in Paris. Damn...

I had no idea where we were—or how to get back to my uncles' house, for that matter—so I was thankful Tasha knew exactly what was waiting for us around each corner. I had to walk fast to keep up with her. She didn't walk, she *strutted*. She moved like she owned the place.

"It's almost September," she said. "There's only a few tourists left." For a second, I thought she'd said *terrorists*. I forced myself to stop fantasizing about life in Europe and to focus on Tasha's every word. *Pay attention, Destiny. Your new BFF is talking to you.* "They'll be gone by the time school starts in two weeks. Then you won't see them again until May."

"What's school like?" I asked.

She gave me a look. "You'll learn to hate it."

"That bad?"

"I've been stuck in a classroom with the same idiots for over ten years now," she said. "That's why I'm glad you're here. I'm sick of knowing everyone."

"How do you know my uncles?"

"I used to work at the Magic Mansion," she said, as if I knew. "Last summer."

"Did you quit?"

"No. I'd never do that. I love that place," she said. "They had to let me go. Business isn't what it used to be. I feel really bad for your uncles. They work really hard. I think they might have to shut the place down soon."

"Really?" I said. "But it seems like such a cool place."

Tasha shrugged. "I guess people don't want magic anymore."

"That's sad."

She stopped in her tracks and touched the sleeve of my sweatshirt. I imagined her fingertips were soft, but I couldn't feel them through the fabric. A thin line of sweat swam down the back of my leg and tickled the inside of my ankle. "So you believe in it, then?" she asked. "You believe in magic?"

"That's strange," I said. "You're the second person to ask me that question today."

"Around here," she said, "that doesn't surprise me."

"Really?"

"Yeah," she said. "I'll explain it on the way."

Tasha was on the move again. I struggled to catch up. "Where are we going?"

"You'll see."

"Okay."

"So," she said, "what's your answer?"

"About believing in magic?" I asked.

She nodded. "Yeah."

I wiped my forehead with the back of my hand. Tasha was right. The humidity in Avalon Cove was awful—even worse than Chicago. I was turning into a human puddle. A sweatshirt? In *August*? What was I thinking? "I don't know if I do," I answered.

"Give it a week or two. Maybe less," she said. "You'll believe."

I thought about asking if we could stop somewhere, maybe dart inside a candle shop or an art gallery to suck up some free air-conditioning. Instead, I smiled and sweated and said, "Well, you know what they say: seeing is believing."

She stopped again. I was grateful for the moment to catch my breath. Clearly I needed to work some cardio into my daily routine if I was going to be friends with Tasha. The girl moved like a train. "So, if I show you some magic, then you'll believe?" she asked.

I exhaled and said, "Um, yeah. I guess so."

"Then as soon as we get to where we're going, I'll prove it to you. Deal?"

I nodded. "Deal."

We were on the move again.

"We're cutting through the park by the harbor," she explained. "It's a shortcut."

"Sure," I said. "Sounds great."

We turned a corner. The park was nothing more than a circle of towering trees, a few redwood picnic tables, and an empty playground. Beyond it—as Tasha had promised—was a beautiful harbor swirling with sailboats, late afternoon Jet

Skiers, and skinny girls in barely existing bikinis. I glanced down at the baggy sweatshirt, two-year-old khaki skirt, and scuffed white sandals I was wearing and admitted to myself I was out of place. This wasn't Lake Michigan. And I would have to do five hundred crunches a night to have a bikini body—by *next* summer.

No more Cheetos. Or double stuffed Oreos. Good-bye Ben & Jerry's. Hello cute boy running toward us.

"Who's that?" I asked not ready to stop staring at him. Even from yards away, I could tell he was adorable.

"That's Topher," Tasha said.

"He's cute," I admitted.

"He's gay," she responded.

"Damn…"

"Get ready," she warned me. "He's in trouble. I can tell."

He reached us within seconds. He grabbed Tasha's arm. She steadied him. "They're after me," he panted. Apparently, Tasha was right. He was scared. He doubled over, and I worried he might throw up.

"All three of them?" Tasha asked him.

"Yes," he said, gasping for air. His cheeks were flushed and his blue-gray eyes were round with fear. "They're right behind me."

Tasha looked in the distance. "I see 'em," she said. "Topher, take Destiny with you. Go to the tunnel and wait for me there. I'll deal with these idiots."

"By yourself?" he asked.

"I can handle it," she assured him. "I always do. Now… go."

Topher looked at me. "Come on," he said. He broke into a run. I had no choice but to do the same. I followed him, struggling to keep up in my flimsy sandals. I was tempted to rip the things off my feet and dash toward the park barefoot. "Hurry!"

He headed back toward the playground, which was surrounded by sand. I rushed past a swing set and a metal slide in time to see Topher scramble into a cement tunnel. It couldn't have been more than six feet in length and was open at both ends. *This* was our hideout? Maybe if we were seven and we were trying to win a game of hide-and-seek, it would be the perfect spot. But this was different. Fearing for our safety, I crawled inside beside him.

"What do we do now?" I asked, breathless.

"We wait," he instructed. "Tasha will let us know when we're safe."

"I take it you've done this before?"

He nodded. "They chase me every day."

I looked at him. "Seriously?"

"Well, maybe not *every* day," he said. "Sometimes I outsmart them. Or I wait until they get bored and go away."

"That's crazy," I said. "Why do they wanna hurt you?"

"Why else?" he said. "Because I'm gay."

I decided I hated my sandals. I slipped them off. "That's the stupidest thing I've ever heard of."

"Tasha says the same thing," he said. "She calls them Neanderthals."

"I can think of a few worse names."

"You're new here," he said, "but we knew you were coming."

"Do you know my uncles?" I asked.

"Know them? They've practically adopted me."

"Yeah," I said, "they seem cool like that. To tell you the truth, I don't really know them very well. I didn't even find out I was moving here until two days ago. A lawyer told me."

"You're really lucky you get to live with them," he said. "My mom works all the time since it's just the two of us, so they feed me and take me places with them a lot. Let me hang out. Talk to me about…stuff."

"Do they know?"

"About me being gay?"

"No, that you get chased every day by a bunch of jerks?"

He shook his head and lowered his eyes. "I haven't told them yet."

"Maybe you should," I said. "Or go to the police."

"What are they going to do about it?"

"Arrest them," I said. "Put them on probation or something like that."

"That won't happen," he said. "Nathan's dad is the captain of the police department."

"So they get away with it? That's insane."

"Tasha says we should just ignore 'em and eventually they'll stop," he told me. "I thought I was gonna be free of 'em until September. I thought summer school would be safe. But no such luck. Nathan flunked algebra, and Skeeter and Boyd will be forty by the time they graduate."

I struggled with the impulse to hug him. Topher and I had known each for exactly five minutes, so I decided not to. I folded my arms across my chest. The cement felt cool against the back of my legs. "Topher, I don't know you very well, but this isn't fair," I said. "You shouldn't have to live in fear."

"Have you seen them?" he asked. "They're twice my size."

Topher *was* a small guy. He was shorter than me, and thin. He was definitely not a jock. He was more *emo*, complete with smudges of black guyliner around his beautiful silvery blue eyes. He had long fingers. I stared at them, wondering if he played piano. His hair was jet black and cut into a jagged mess. He was wearing a ripped pair of black jeans, a striped blue and white T-shirt, and a pair of red Converse.

"What are you?" I asked. "A skater? Punk? Emo? Goth?"

"I'm just me," he answered. "Maybe a little bit of everything."

I smiled. "I like that."

"Destiny?" he said. "No offense, but…you seem *way* too pretty to hang out with us."

I almost laughed. "Are you kidding me?"

"You look like you play volleyball," he said. "Are you a model? You know, runway?"

Topher's assessment of me sounded genuine, which made him more endearing.

"Topher, I think that's the sweetest thing a guy's ever said to me," I said.

"Adrianna was right," he said. "You're perfect."

"For what?" I asked.

"You'll see," he answered.

What's up with the people on this island? Everyone is so secretive and cryptic.

"And Adrianna?" I asked. "Is she a friend of yours, too?"

He grinned. "You could say that. She's the one who told us you were coming. She knew before your uncles did," he said. "Even before your mom died."

A hand reached inside the tunnel. I almost screamed and clutched Topher's arm, nearly crawling into his lap. Tasha knelt down in the sand and poked her head inside.

"The coast is clear," she said. She straightened her yellow headband and motioned for us to get out of the tunnel. I slid out first. Tasha offered a hand and helped me up. I wiped the back of my skirt, hoping I didn't have sand stuck to the back of my thighs.

I'll never wear a skirt again. At least not when I'm hanging out with these two.

"How'd you get rid of 'em this time?" Topher asked.

"How do you think?" Tasha said. "I threatened to put a curse on them."

"Again?"

She nodded. "Of course. They still think I'm a witch."

Topher turned to me. "That reminds me," he said. "Destiny, do you believe in magic?"

I gave them both a look. "Okay," I said, a hand on my hip. "What's the deal? Why does everyone keep asking me that?"

Tasha reached out and brushed a few strands of hair away from my eyes. "Because here," she said, "you either believe in magic...or you don't. Topher and I...we believe."

"We need to know where you stand," Topher echoed.

"Where I stand?" I repeated. "I'm standing on an island in South Carolina a thousand miles from home."

Topher slid his arm around my waist. He whispered into my ear, "That life is behind you now."

I started to cry, and felt like a complete idiot. "I know," I said, with a small nod. "I can never go back."

"We know what you've been through," Tasha said. She took my hand and placed it in hers. Her skin was as soft and velvety as it looked. "We know about pain."

I looked around, worried people might be staring at the three of us. The playground was empty. Except for the seagulls gliding in the air above.

My voice cracked when I spoke. "I miss my mom," I admitted. It was the first time I'd said the words. Just saying them made me cry even harder.

Damn it. Stop crying. You're such an idiot.

"She misses you, too," Tasha said, tightening her grip on my hand.

"Soon everything will make sense," Topher promised.

I shook my head. "No…it won't," I said. "I don't understand why she had to die."

"Because," he said, "it brought you here to Avalon Cove."

"To us," Tasha added. "Everything happens for a reason."

"You guys are being super sweet and I really appreciate that," I said, "especially since you don't even know me. I swear I'm not usually an emotional mess like this."

"We want to take you somewhere," Topher said.

"Okay," I said. "But should I call my uncles first? Do either one of you have a cell phone I can borrow? I left mine in Chicago. I figured it was time for a fresh start. And a new phone."

"I promised Sir Frederic the Great I'd have you home by nine," Tasha reminded me. "And you will be."

Tasha and Topher pulled away from me, stepping aside. They gave each other a strange look and started walking away, leaving the playground—and me—behind.

I followed.

"I only have one question," I said, once I caught up with them.

"You can ask us anything," Topher said. "We have nothing to hide."

"Where exactly are we going?" I asked.

Tasha smiled at me and said, "We're taking you to Wonderland."

CHAPTER TWO

"This place gives me the creeps," I said, standing outside what I assumed was a haunted house. I shivered.

The three of us were shoulder to shoulder, with me in the middle.

"How can you say that?" Topher replied. "Isn't it the most beautiful thing you've ever seen?"

I looked at him. His blue eyes were filled with wonder and awe. *Are we seeing the same thing?*

The gray house was old and weathered. It loomed above us, stretching up toward the darkening sky. The face of the house was covered with dark windows in a variety of shapes. There was an archway above the wide, wooden porch. Even though it had a quaint miniature roof above, the entrance to the house still seemed evil—like a hungry mouth, ready to swallow us alive.

I glanced up to the rounded tower shooting up from the roof. I wondered if some poor girl was being held hostage up there, praying for us to storm the house and rescue her.

"I agree with the whole *beauty is in the eye of the beholder* thing, but this place looks haunted," I told them. "It's straight out of a horror film—like a serial killer lives here."

"It's a historical landmark. It's Victorian," he explained. "They call it a Queen Anne."

I folded my arms across my chest. "I call it an eyesore," I replied.

I stared at the house again. Decay had set in long ago and the place looked on the verge of collapse. The landscape was dead, adding to the macabre ambience. It was obvious the place had been abandoned years ago.

"You have to remember," Tasha said to Topher, "Destiny hasn't been inside yet. This is her first time here."

"Oh yeah," Topher said. "I forgot."

"What do you mean?" I asked her.

"Wonderland's not the same for you yet," she said. "To the outsider's eye, this place looks…a certain way."

"Yeah," I said. "It looks like it should be condemned."

"But to us," she said, "it looks like the most beautiful place we've ever seen."

I gave her a look of disbelief. I may have even rolled my eyes. "What are you talking about?" I asked. "Are you hearing what you're saying to me? Because it doesn't make any sense."

"I know how it sounds," Tasha agreed. "But it's true, Destiny."

It'd been a long day, a long two weeks. All I wanted to do was slip into a hot bath, crawl into my new bed, and bring my first day in Avalon Cove to a finish. Agitation slipped into my voice. My words were coated with my growing frustration. "What you're telling me isn't *possible*," I said.

"Yes, it is," Topher said, "because we believe."

"Believe whatever you want. I don't get it," I answered.

"You will," Tasha assured me.

I turned my back to the house and faced the quiet street. The air felt suspended, motionless, like we were trapped inside a photograph.

Like we were the only people alive.

"The first time we came here, we saw it the same way you do," Topher said. "It probably looks old and scary."

"Um...because it *is*."

He smiled at me and said, "But once you go inside—"

Tasha jumped in. "Once you cross over the threshold—"

"Nothing will be the same for you again," he said. "I promise you, Destiny. You won't regret it."

"Whatever you two smoked or inhaled...I don't want any. Okay?"

"You think we're crazy?" Tasha asked with a grin.

"No, I think you're high. Or someone has brainwashed the two of you," I said. "I'm not interested in joining some crazy cult, so I think I should go now. I'm outta here."

Tasha's words touched the back of my neck. "He wants to meet you," she said.

"Who does?" I asked with an irritated shrug.

"Dominic," she continued. "Adrianna told us so. He's inside."

"He's been waiting for you," Topher added. "We all have."

I spun back around and faced them. Enough was enough. Clearly, it was Pick on the New Girl Day and I was in no mood to be anyone's punch line. "Listen, don't take this the wrong way because you both seem like cool people, but if you think I'm going inside, you're both out of your minds. I'm sorry you brought me all this way. I'm tired and I'm worn out. I'm hungry and I need sleep. Now, either take me home or point me in the right direction," I said. "It's getting dark and I want to go home now." They both stared at me blankly.

"We'll take you home, Destiny," Tasha said. "But will you go inside with us first?"

"Just once," Topher urged.

"We promise that nothing bad will happen to you," she said. "You'll be safe."

"You'll be happy you did, once you go through with it," he added.

"Fine!" I said, exasperated. "I'll do it. But both of you are coming inside with me."

"Deal," Tasha agreed. She stepped forward and pushed open the wrought-iron gate. It creaked like it hadn't been touched in decades—maybe even a century.

As we started moving across the cracked cement walkway leading us to the house, Tasha and Topher each slipped an arm through mine. They were either offering me some comfort and encouragement, or ensuring I wouldn't be able to escape. We moved in unison—a single unit, creeping closer to the nightmarish house.

We climbed the wooden front steps to the dilapidated porch. I feared the wood would split beneath our feet and the house would devour us whole. The shredded screen door was hanging from one hinge. I wondered if someone had broken it fleeing for their life. I could tell the wooden front door had once been beautiful, but now it was splintered and marred. To the left of the door was a faded ceramic placard with the word "Wonderland" hand-painted on it, in flowery and inviting script. The first "o" in the word was missing and had been replaced with a heart, scrawled in either red ink or lipstick. I stared at the word and heard myself say aloud, "This is Wonderland?"

"It is," Topher said. His soft words tickled my ear. "You'll see."

Tasha reached out and pressed the tarnished brass doorbell. It gonged and chimed, deep and sad. "Are you ready?" she asked me.

I nodded. "I really don't have a choice," I said.

There was a clicking sound and the front door slowly opened. I had no idea who—or *what*—was on the other side. My heart beat quickened with anticipation. I licked my lips and swallowed the lump of fear in my throat.

"Here we go," Tasha said. I could hear the smile in her voice.

We crossed the threshold, stepping into the house. We disappeared into a sea of pitch-black darkness.

I heard the door click closed behind us.

I held my hand up in front of my face. Nothing.

I knew I sounded scared. "I can't see anything," I said. My voice reverberated around us.

Are we in a tunnel? What's happening to me?

"It takes a second," Tasha assured me.

I reached for her hand and squeezed it.

"We're making the transition," Topher explained. "You might feel a little strange."

Just as he said it, I felt a blast of warm air in my face. It smelled fragrant, like flowers. White carnations. I could taste them on my lips.

I closed my eyes. A rush of adrenaline surged through me. It was like neon stars were sparkling beneath my skin. I trembled from a particularly intense crest of euphoria. Even though I could feel solid ground beneath my feet, I had the sensation I was falling—or spinning. Maybe I was doing both.

Is the floor moving?

My emotions began intensifying. It was as if layers of joy were wrapping around my soul. It was a beautiful sensation. The sweetness made me think of walking outside our Chicago apartment on the first day of spring, when the snow had melted and the city was reemerging, having survived another winter. I could almost feel the warm sun on my skin. I inhaled deeply, intoxicated by the fresh blossoms that must be floating in the ink-black air around me.

The wave of happiness reminded me of being a child again and falling asleep in the backseat of my parents' car. I could hear them whispering in the front, their words still full of love for one another. I knew once we got home and pulled into our driveway, my father would scoop me up in his arms and carry me upstairs to my bedroom.

Maybe it was Christmas Eve. In the morning, we would be together again. The three of us. Before my brother was born. Before the divorce. The sickness. The funeral.

The world seemed so simple then.

All of the sadness I felt for my mother's death disappeared, washed away. I was now engulfed with an overwhelming sense that everything was going to be all right, that life was normal again.

I tightened my grip on Tasha's hand, certain she would cry out in pain at any second.

Her voice cut through the dark. "We're almost there," she promised.

I heard music then. It was soft at first, like a faraway lullaby, and it grew closer. It was tiptoeing toward me from all directions. For a second, I felt like I'd crawled inside a music box. I was pirouetting in ballet slippers and a pink tutu in my mind, moving in circles with my mother's grace.

The haunting piano vibrated inside me, stirring a bitter sweetness. The music calmed and exhilarated me at the same time. I felt invincible and nostalgic. I wasn't sure if I wanted to dance or cry.

I recognized the music at once. My mother used to dance to it in our living room. With my eyes shut tight, I could see the moment, only the colors were more vibrant. The textures of the memory begged to be touched: her soft rose-colored skirt, her smooth hands, the shiny wooden floors. I was much younger. It was before my mother had opened the dance studio on Belmont Avenue. It was before the cancer.

It was Beethoven.

The music made me smile. I allowed myself to linger in the memory, reaching out for my mother's hand, wanting to touch her, to feel my fingertips against her palm. I knew she wasn't there, but the moment felt so *real.*

She pulled away from me and continued to dance. I watched her feet, gliding across the floor of our living room. We were in the house on Armitage Avenue. My father hadn't lost his job yet. My mother still had light in her eyes.

A stranger's voice entered the memory, my thoughts. It came to me from the center of the darkness.

"Do you recognize the music?" a woman asked me, her voice soft and warm. It was inviting. I felt safe and secure. The gentleness in her tone made me feel loved. There was something very familiar about her voice, but I couldn't place it.

"Yes," I answered. "I do."

The woman and I spoke in unison, saying *Moonlight Sonata* at the same time.

My muscles had relaxed. Any tension I'd been carrying in my body was gone. I felt light-headed, but not dizzy.

"You may open your eyes now, Destiny," she said.

I blinked and stared in awe.

Where am I?

I was standing in the foyer of a beautiful home, surrounded by an array of expensive-looking antiques. In front of me was a wooden staircase leading up to a second floor. My eyes focused in on the banister. It looked hand carved, with giant stars and loopy swirls etched into it.

I looked from one side to the other. No sign of Tasha or Topher. Just pools of golden sunlight pouring in from every window, washing the shiny wooden floors in a bath of pure, warm rays.

I turned around in a slow circle, trying to take it all in: a sparkling chandelier above me; vases of beautiful flowers sitting on every flat surface; gorgeous cherry and mahogany furniture and plush wingback chairs; stunning paintings in gilt frames hanging from the walls; a grandfather clock chiming behind me; a grand piano in the far corner of the front room, begging to be played.

It was picture perfect, inviting and comfortable. Already, I never wanted to leave.

Had I somehow stepped back into time? It certainly seemed that way. From where I stood by the staircase, surrounded by open doorways on every side, I had a strong sense of the past. Had I somehow tripped back into a yesteryear? Was that even possible?

I heard a scratching sound repeating over and over. Something was stuck and needed my help. The music was being played on an old phonograph, situated on a wooden stand not far from the grandfather clock next to me in the foyer. I reached down, lifted the heavy brass arm, and moved the needle away from the spinning vinyl. I tried to turn the machine off, but there was no button or plug.

How does this thing work?

"You have to wind it up to make it play," the woman's voice said.

I looked up and saw her standing about twenty feet away from me, in the doorway of a room walled with books. My breath stopped. She looked like an angel, dressed in a loose-fitting tunic made of white material that sparkled lightly when she moved. Her hair was platinum and pulled up off her neck. Large curls hung around her face. Just as I'd thought, she was much older than me. I couldn't be certain of her age.

"You look like a goddess," I heard myself say.

She smiled at me and laughed a little. "You're a sweet girl," she said, "but I'm no goddess."

"You're not?" I said, hoping my shaky smile didn't reveal how nervous I felt. Her presence was powerful and commanding, yet not intimidating. I had the impression I was talking to someone very important. "Are you sure?"

"I'm Adrianna," she said. "Adrianna Marveaux." She reached out a hand in my direction. "Welcome to Wonderland."

I stepped toward her and accepted her hand in mine. Her skin felt like silk. She squeezed my palm and fingers, looked into my eyes, and said, "Destiny, I've waited for this moment for a very long time."

For some reason, I started to blush. "Thank you, Mrs. Marveaux."

She touched my cheek. I winced a little from the physical contact. "You may call me Adrianna." Her voice was smooth and gentle. I wondered how many men had fallen in love with her just from the first word she spoke to them.

"All right," I said with a slight nod. "It's very nice to meet you, Adrianna. I'm Destiny Moore. From Chicago."

She smiled and laughed again. It was a sweet sound, like yellow ribbons of happiness were streaming out of her mouth. "I know," she said. "I know everything about you."

"Have we met before?" I asked.

She was holding both of my hands. We stood face-to-face. I was slightly taller. "Almost," she answered. "Once. But fate intervened."

"Is that why I'm here now?" I asked. "To meet you?"

She shrugged a little. "Among other reasons."

"Then can you tell me where I am exactly?"

There were a few tiny lines around her green eyes.

They were the only indication of her age. She wore a lot of makeup—heavy blush, glittery eye shadow, fake eyelashes, and red lipstick. Yet she didn't look cheap or cartoonish. She exuded sophistication and allure. I still felt like I knew her. She seemed so familiar. I wanted to ask if she'd been in a movie or maybe on TV.

"Don't you know where you are?" she asked me.

I shook my head. "All Tasha and Topher would tell me is that they wanted me to see this place before I went home," I said. "I mean, to where my two uncles live."

"But you were really tired and worn out from your trip. You didn't want to come," she reminded me.

"Yes," I agreed. "It's true. I still don't know where I am."

"You know this is a place called Wonderland."

"Um…yeah…I saw the sign out front."

"And Tasha and Topher—they told you about this."

"Yes, but what is it?" I lifted up on my toes to peer over her shoulder, into the room behind her. "Just a big, beautiful, old house?"

"That and so much more," she said. "I own this place. I have for many years."

"It's very lovely."

She put a hand on her hip and gave me a playful look. "I seem to recall you didn't care much for the outside."

I felt embarrassed. Had she heard the awful things I'd said about the house? "No offense," I said, "but from the curb, this place looks spooky."

"In due time, it will grow on you. It might seem different to you on your second visit."

She stepped away from me. I could smell her intoxicating perfume floating behind her as she moved deeper into the high-ceilinged room. Immediately, I followed. I glanced up and felt a little dizzy, overwhelmed by the grandness of the library. I'd never seen so many books in one house.

Adrianna glided down into a chaise cushioned with deep red fabric. She reclined on her side like Cleopatra waiting for manservants to peel her some grapes.

"Will I be coming back here again?" I asked.

Adrianna motioned with a delicate wave for me to sit down across from her, on the opposite side of a beautiful knee-high mahogany coffee table. "That depends," she said.

I sank into a gold velvet love seat. "On what?" I asked.

"On you," she said.

This love seat is so comfortable, I want to curl up and go to sleep right now.

There was a sterling silver tea set sitting on the table between us. She leaned forward and lifted the teapot. She filled two cups. They were pale yellow porcelain with purple grapes and green leaves painted on the sides of them.

"Well, I like it here," I said, "so far."

"Destiny, the best is yet to come," she assured me. "You haven't met Dominic yet."

"Who is he?"

"He's everything you've ever imagined," she explained. "I think he's the one for you."

"The one?" I repeated.

"Yes," she said, "but I'll let you decide for yourself."

I gave her a look. "Tasha and Topher brought me here just to meet a guy?"

She shook her head. "No...he's no ordinary man."

She dropped two sugar cubes into each cup, added milk from a miniature silver pitcher, and stirred each in turn with a tiny silver spoon. She offered me a cup and saucer.

My hands trembled slightly when I took the teacup from

her. The delicate saucer rattled a little against the bottom of the cup. I glanced down. The liquid inside the cup sparkled like a dash of diamond dust had been added to it. "And this is no ordinary place, is it?" I asked.

"It never has been," she said.

"It seems so big."

"It is," she said. "Five bedrooms in all."

"Wow," I said. "You must have a big family."

She took a small sip of the glittery tea and said, "You can think of Wonderland as a boarding house of sorts."

"Like a bed-and-breakfast inn?" I asked.

She tilted her head a little. "You could call it that," she said with a slight shrug. "Guests come here from all over. They visit awhile. Then…they move on."

"They come to Avalon Cove, just to stay here?" I asked.

"They each have a different reason for being here. For what brings them to me."

"Do you have many guests now?" I asked.

"At the moment, just three," she said. "Dominic arrived last month. He's been very distraught. I know you'll be good for him, for his heart. Juliet and Pablo have been here for at least two weeks. Since the day before Tasha and Topher discovered Wonderland."

"Will they be staying much longer?"

"Very soon I will explain everything to you," she said. "I promise."

"Is that a polite way to tell me to mind my own business?"

"No. You're quite curious. You always have been. I imagine that's why you're here."

"My best friend back home—her name's Samantha—she says I ask too many questions."

"I think a person can never ask enough," Adrianna said.

"That's really nice of you to say. Still…I'm not really sure what I'm doing here."

"You're wondering if this is all real, aren't you?"

"I feel like I've been hallucinating since I stepped off the plane a few hours ago. The Magic Mansion. The island. This place."

"It can be a bit much," she agreed. "Avalon Cove is very unique."

"My mother grew up here," I said.

"Yes, I know."

"Did you know my mother?" I asked, somehow already knowing what her answer would be.

"Very well."

"Did you know that she died? She had cancer."

Adrianna lowered her eyes to her teacup. "Yes."

"I miss her very much," I said, filling up with sadness. "I don't know what I'm going to do without her, to be honest with you."

"Here," she said, "you'll find there's no reason for sorrow."

"That's impossible," I said.

"Is it?" she asked.

"Everyone gets sad at some point in their life," I said. "It just happens."

"I see," she answered before taking another sip of tea.

I looked up to the ceiling then. I heard heavy footsteps. Someone was running across the floor above us. The chandelier vibrated.

"Where are my friends?" I asked.

"They're out in the garden. Playing a very competitive game of croquet, I believe."

"Then who's upstairs?" I asked. "Your husband?"

"A new guest has arrived," she said. "Directly above us is the arrival station."

I stood up. "I need to go home soon."

Adrianna placed her cup and saucer on the table and lowered her transparent shoes to the hardwood floor. "You'll be there in a few minutes," she assured me. "Just in time for meatloaf and game shows."

My eyes moved to the open doorway of the room we were in. "Maybe I should tell Tasha and Topher that it's time to go."

I saw something was moving slowly across the floor from the corner of my eye. It was an overweight orange cat. It rubbed up against Adrianna and flicked its tail. "Don't mind him," she said. "He thinks he owns the place."

He gazed up at me with his golden eyes. It looked like he was smiling. "He seems very sweet," I said, temporarily forgetting about my desire to leave. "Did he just smile at me?"

"He does that sometimes. His name is Montgomery," she said, "and he is sweet. In fact, I can safely say that he's the nicest gentleman I've ever met. Other than my husband Alfred."

"Can you explain something to me?"

"Destiny, I assume I'll be explaining many things to you," she said. She stood up.

"Yes, you probably will," I said. "If I start to annoy you, just let me know. I'm curious…right before the three of us walked into your house, the sun was setting outside. Sitting here, there's so much sunlight around us. Like it's the middle of the day."

She smiled. "We prefer sunlight here at Wonderland," she

said. "Occasionally, the mood calls for a starry night. Speaking of which…I would like to give you an invitation."

We moved toward to the doorway of the library. "An invitation?" I repeated.

"Yes," she said. "For tomorrow evening. I'm assuming you'll be free."

"I don't know. My uncles might—"

"You will be," she said. "I've already made sure of it."

"Then I'll be here," I said "What time?"

"No need to worry about time," she said with a smile. "You'll know exactly when to arrive, Destiny. You won't be late."

"Can you tell me what the occasion is?" I asked.

"I'm having a dinner party," she said. "In your honor, of course."

"For me?" I said. "But why?"

"Why not?" she asked. "You don't think you deserve a dinner party?"

"I've never been to one before," I explained.

"I know," she said. "You'll want a new dress to wear. I have it on good authority that Dominic's favorite color is cobalt blue. It's a strange shade, if you ask me. But…I guess I can see the appeal. It's very bright. Very commanding. Most men like red. But not him. Dominic is very different." She looked me in the eye. "There's only one dress in Avalon Cove in that color in your size. Ask Clark to take you shopping tomorrow. He'll know the place to go."

We were back in the foyer, standing beneath the grand chandelier, at the bottom of the staircase.

"Can I ask you a question?" I asked.

She smiled at me again. "I was expecting you to," she said. "Go on."

"Why are you doing this? I mean, why are you being so nice to me?"

Her light green eyes sparkled as she looked up at me and said, "I've waited a very long time to meet you. Allow me to spoil you. You're a remarkable young woman."

"I am?"

She placed a fingertip against my lips to silence me. "Yes, you are," she continued. "You have a beautiful soul and a big heart. You've loved a lot and never received enough in return. This is my moment to do something for you. To give you a chance at true love."

I smiled at her. "I'd be happy with just a dinner party," I said. "Really. I swear."

"That's what I admire about you the most," she said. "You've always made do with whatever came your way. You're not like most people, Destiny. You're one of the few who can truly make the best out of any situation."

"You're wrong about one thing, though," I said.

"I am?" she asked.

"You said I've never received a lot of love, but I have," I explained.

She reached around me and placed a hand over the brass knob of the front door. "What do you mean?" she asked.

I heard them again: footsteps above us. I lifted my eyes to the ceiling, to the rattling crystal teardrops of the chandelier. I listened for a second to the pattern of the movement, the rhythm. I realized that whoever was upstairs wasn't walking or running: they were dancing.

A door opened on the second floor. Bright light flooded the top of the staircase, illuminating the area with a stark white glow. Specks of silver glitter floated in the air. I saw a figure step into the beams.

"My mother…" I heard myself say. "She loved me more than anyone."

I saw the jazz shoe on the top step, then another, and the pleated hemline of a rose-colored skirt. And I knew…

"It's time for you to go now," Adrianna said. She opened the front door. I felt her hand, firm on my lower back. She spun me away from the staircase to face the open doorway—a wall of darkness.

"Wait!" I begged.

"It's too soon," she insisted. "You have to meet Dominic first."

"Is it her?" I demanded.

"Go now, Destiny!"

"Is it her?!"

In response, Adrianna shoved me into the pit of blackness. I heard the door slam shut behind me and the sound rumbled in my ears. Within seconds, the haunting opening chords of Beethoven's *Moonlight Sonata* filled the vast space around me.

I concentrated on the melody in the music, knowing I was already moving fast.

I closed my eyes as I drifted further away from Wonderland, falling back to my new undiscovered life in Avalon Cove.

I was spiraling back to reality.

CHAPTER THREE

When I opened my eyes, I was standing on a wooden front porch facing a white screen door. I didn't know where I was, but hoped it was my new home.

I looked up. A mosquito buzzed and banged against the glass shade covering the hazy yellow porch light. The insect seemed lost and confused.

I knew *exactly* how it felt.

I glanced around and inspected my surroundings. From what I could tell, whoever lived here loved ceramic pigs and either spent a considerable amount of time perfecting their front lawn and white roses, or paid someone to do it for them.

Exhausted, I was tempted to crawl onto the wooden porch swing and wait until morning to ring the doorbell.

I had no idea how I ended up here. I remembered leaving Wonderland and stepping into a sea of darkness. It seemed like only a split second had passed before I had arrived here.

I have no idea what time it is. Should I knock? Ring the bell? Run away?

I pressed down on the metal handle of the screen door and it clicked. I pulled it open and knocked on the front door. I heard footsteps approaching.

The door opened. "Destiny?" It was Clark. He had a dish towel draped over one shoulder. He was wearing a pair of gray sweats and a faded Violent Femmes concert T-shirt. His brown hair was messy. I was tempted to reach out and smooth it back down into place. I could hear a television on somewhere in the distance and the familiar voice of Alex Trebek.

I tried unsuccessfully to hide my relief I was in the right place. I beamed at him like a dork.

Great. It's your first night here and already they're going to think you're high or drunk—or both. Stop smiling, you idiot.

"It's good to see you," I said. "It's been a while."

He gave me a strange look. "You don't have to knock," he said with a soft smile.

I reached for the knob on the front door and jiggled it. "No?"

I could hear the concern in his voice. "No…you live here now," he said. "This is your home, too."

I felt nervous and weird. I didn't know what to do with my hands. I slid them into the front pockets of my sweatshirt. "I didn't want to…bother you," I offered.

He stepped aside, opened the door wider, and gestured from me to come in. I took a step and entered my new home. I could tell my uncles had lived there for a long time. The two-story house wasn't cluttered, but it wasn't exactly organized either.

Clark touched my arm. "Are you okay?"

I looked into his friendly eyes. "Yeah, I'm fine," I said. "Just…really tired. Long day."

"Are you sure?" he asked. "I mean, if you need to talk…"

I was tempted to hug him. I wanted him to hug me back and tell me I was okay. That what I'd just experienced in a place called Wonderland wasn't some drug-induced hallucination, and I wasn't insane.

"That's super sweet, but I'm cool," I said.

He shut the door behind us and turned the deadbolt. "Hungry?" he asked.

I inhaled deeply. The house smelled like a comforting combination of home-cooked food, cinnamon, and fresh-cut flowers. "I'm starving, actually," I confessed.

He looked surprised. "Tasha didn't feed you?"

Oh my God...Tasha. Where was she? And Topher? Did they stay at Wonderland? I'm a horrible friend for leaving them behind. They're gonna hate me already.

"No," I said, hoping my sudden panic didn't show. "I had some tea earlier."

"Hot tea?"

I nodded. "Peppermint tea."

"Wow," he said. "I used to drink that in college."

"I forgot my watch," I explained. "And I need to get a cell phone. What time is it?"

"It's almost eight," he answered.

"I was worried I was going to be late."

"Your Uncle Fred will be happy you're home. He'll never admit it, but he was worried about you," he said. "You can go in and say hi to him if you want, while I warm you up a plate of food. He's in the living room. He's probably still high."

I blinked at his words. "What?"

Clark laughed a little. "He loves Vanna White. He's obsessed with her," he explained, grinning. "For an hour after the show's over, he's high on love."

"Vanna White?" I repeated. "Really?"

"I've put up with it for years," Clark said. "If he were straight, I'd be worried. I take comfort in the fact that I make him watch *Jeopardy* with me and I swoon over Alex Trebek every chance I get, just to even the score."

"You guys are adorable," I said.

Clark gestured toward the living room with his thumb.

"Go tell Sir Frederic that. Maybe he'll believe you. He thinks he's old."

"Um…he is," I said, still grinning like a fool. "That's why I'm happy he has you…I mean, *us*."

Clark disappeared to the kitchen. I walked into the living room. I found my uncle buried beneath a tattered quilt in a brown leather recliner. I recognized the shoddy craftsmanship immediately.

"Did my grandmother make that quilt for you?" I asked. Each time she visited us in Chicago, she would always bring us samples of her latest craft craze. We'd had closets full of quilts, embroidered pillows, macramé plant holders, scrapbooks, creepy dolls, and crocheted blankets.

Uncle Fred looked up at me. "She did, actually," he said. "She thought she was…domestic."

"But she really wasn't," I said. "We all just let her think she was. Whenever Grandma came to see us in Chicago, my mom did everything in her power to keep Grandma away from the stove. I think she was worried the apartment might catch on fire."

Uncle Fred smiled at me. I thought of my mother. They had similar features. I knew they hadn't been close. I didn't really know why. I'd never thought to ask. "Exactly," he said. "I keep this quilt because it's all I have left of her."

I sat down on a brown leather sofa. I thought about taking off my sandals. My feet were killing me. "Do you miss her?" I asked.

His eyes shifted back to the television. "I miss everyone," he said. "I've lost a lot of people."

I leaned back into the sofa, feeling my body start to relax. A hot shower was calling my name. Just as soon as I devoured a plate of whatever it was that smelled so amazing in the kitchen.

I looked at my uncle, studying his profile. I wondered what he looked like without a mustache. I couldn't remember ever seeing him without one.

I wanted to tell him he didn't need to wear the silly-looking toupée. He should just accept aging gracefully and go *au naturel*.

My eyes drifted down to his hands. They looked weathered.

"How many people have you lost?" I heard myself ask.

He shrugged slightly, as if his shoulders were heavy. "More than I care to count," he said. "Be happy you're still young, Destiny."

"I miss her, too," I said. "Grandma…and my mom."

Uncle Fred was silent for a moment before he spoke. He cleared his throat and said, "I know this has to be hard on you. You've had one heckuva tough time."

"It's not that bad," I said, surprised by the tears filling my eyes. "Being here with you and Clark."

"I want you to feel like this is your home," he said. "I want you to love Avalon Cove just as much as we do."

I thought about Wonderland, and all the strange, unexplainable things I'd encountered there. I wanted to know more about Adrianna Marveaux. Had my time there been real? A dream? Some weird illusion? Was I going crazy?

I wanted to meet Dominic since he and I were perfect for each other—according to almost everyone I'd met during my first day in South Carolina.

I made a mental note to remind myself to ask Clark to take me dress shopping tomorrow. If the dinner party Adrianna was planning really *was* in my honor, I wanted to look my best.

"I think I'm really going to like it here," I told Uncle Fred. "With time."

He fell silent again for a few seconds. "I was surprised…

about your mother's will…about Clark and I becoming your legal guardians."

I stood up then. I went to his chair. I bent down. I kissed my uncle's cheek. "I'm not," I whispered to him. "My mother knew exactly where I belonged."

❖

Are you kidding me?

That was my initial thought when I saw my new attic-converted bedroom. Everything except the carpet was pink.

Clark, who was standing behind me in the doorway, must've read my mind. I felt his palm, reassuring and gentle, land delicately between my shoulder blades.

"You have to forgive your uncle," he said. "He still thinks you're seven. And I secretly suspect he's always wanted a little girl."

"It's sweet," I said with as much sincerity as I could muster.

I felt like I was standing in the middle of a giant wad of bubble gum.

"You hate it, don't you?" Clark asked.

I moved toward the pink canopy bed and sat down on the edge of the pink satin bedspread. I glanced down at the pink pillows. The cases were embroidered with glittery words like "diva" and "princess." I was neither. Couldn't they tell?

"No…it's nice," I said, too tired to fake a smile. "Really."

"We can change it," he offered. "Together."

"Okay," I nodded, hoping my mini-burst of enthusiasm didn't show. "When?"

"This weekend?"

"Sure," I agreed.

"We can make it a little more…"

"Subtle?" I suggested.

He laughed a little. "You poor thing," he said. "You'll probably have nightmares sleeping in this room."

"No worries," I said, picking up one of a dozen stuffed animals. "I have this unicorn to keep me safe." My eyes moved to an electric socket in the wall. "And a Tinker Bell night-light in case I get scared."

"He means well."

"I know," I said. "And I appreciate it. I guess…it'll just take some time for the three of us to get to know each other better. We're not strangers—"

"But we might as well be," Clark finished.

"You won me over with the meatloaf," I confessed. "Where'd you learn to cook like that?"

"Once upon a time I had dreams of going to culinary school," he told me.

"So, what happened?"

He leaned against the door frame and folded his arms across his chest. "Your Uncle Fred happened," he answered. "From the first night I spent in Avalon Cove, I knew this was where I needed to be. This was the life I wanted."

I kicked off my sandals and wiggled my toes. I didn't know what to say to Clark. All I could come up with was: "Oh."

He stepped further in the room. I followed his eyes up to the slanted ceilings. I wondered how long it would be before I ended up with a concussion. One wrong leap out of bed and I'd be knocked out cold.

"I think we forgot how tall you are," he said.

"Maybe it's my fault," I offered. "I was wearing flats at the funeral."

"He thought you'd like it up here better. More privacy."

"So this isn't a ploy to lock me away in the attic?" I asked, smiling. "Should I change my name to what's-her-face from *Jane Eyre*?"

"I don't know who that is," Clark answered. "But you have a private staircase and most importantly..." He moved to a closed door and, in his best Vanna White impression, flung it open. "A private bathroom!"

"That makes it all worth it," I said. "I feel like I just won something."

"I'll let you get settled in," he told me. He leaned down and his soft lips brushed across my cheek. The sensation made my skin tingle. "Sweet dreams, Destiny."

Within seconds Clark was gone, leaving me alone in my pink-ensconced solitude.

I turned toward the window beside my bed. I pulled back a pink chiffon curtain and stared down at the front lawn, the ceramic pigs, and the white roses, sleeping in the dull glow of the misty porch light.

This view was so different from the brick wall my bedroom window in Chicago faced. Even though I was happy to be in Avalon Cove and life seemed like it would be okay for me there, I was already homesick.

I thought about calling Samantha, but remembered I had no cell phone.

I thought about creeping down the private staircase to the kitchen and tiptoeing to the den where I could jump on Clark's laptop just to find out what the rest of the world was doing, since everything in mine was changing by the second.

Instead I just sat on the bed clutching a synthetic unicorn in my arms like I was some sad orphan left in the care of torturous nuns.

Finally, I broke out of my cocoon of self-pity, stood up, and poked my head into the bathroom.

"Yes!" I said, feeling victorious for the first time since I'd stepped off the plane.

The bathroom was straight out of an old movie. It had a clawfoot tub, marble sink, black and white tiled floor, and a small window offering a shoreline view.

Immediately I began making a mental shopping list. I needed candles. I needed bubble bath. I needed about two weeks alone in this glorious bathroom, hidden away from the world.

I pulled back the shower curtain, reached for the silver X-shaped knobs, and turned the water on. Just the sound of it made my body relax. Within seconds, steam drifted up into my face. I felt the tension in my shoulder blades vanish.

I went back to the bedroom, unzipped a suitcase, dug out an oversized T-shirt and a pair of clean underwear, and returned to my newly discovered oasis. I swept my hand across the steam-covered mirror and almost shrieked at the sight of my reflection. I looked beyond hideous. I had dark circles under my eyes. My mascara was slightly smeared. My hair was such a mess and my ponytail was so crooked, I looked like I should be on my way to rehab.

Seconds later, I sank into the porcelain tub of hot water and was overwhelmed by the instant tranquility I felt. Immediately, I closed my eyes.

If only I had some Adele or Duffy to listen to, this moment would be perfect.

Visions of my first day in Avalon Cove started flashing through my mind, like a revolving slide show of postcards. The Magic Mansion and its strange spaceship shape. Tasha and her pastel purple fingernails. Hiding with Topher in the cement tunnel in the park. Adrianna Marveaux's platinum hair and glittery cheeks. My mother's feet on the stairs.

I knew it was her. I could sense it. I felt it the second I saw her jazz shoes and the pleats in her favorite skirt.

Maybe that's why Adrianna had been so quick to make me leave. For some reason, she didn't want me to see my mother.

But how could that be possible? How could my mother be a new guest at Wonderland?

She was dead.

❖

"I know the perfect place to take you," Clark told me the next morning while we were sitting at the kitchen table. He gave the piece of toast he was holding a slight shake and crumbs drifted down to his plate.

I swallowed a mouthful of pancakes before reminding him, "It has to be cobalt blue."

He nodded. "I remember seeing a dress that color in the store window last week at Bettina's. It's a boutique. Cute place. Wacky owner," he said. He looked at me. "Why that color? I mean, with your skin tone you could get away with wearing any shade—but cobalt blue? That's so…*specific.*"

He was right. This wasn't Prom or Homecoming. I wasn't trying to color-coordinate my dress with my date's tie or cummerbund.

"I think the dinner party has a theme," I said quickly, eyes on my plate. "I just…really want to make a good first impression…since I'll be living here now."

Adrianna had been right. Just as she'd told me he would, Clark knew exactly where to take me to buy the dress.

"Look at you," he said, grinning. "Haven't even been in town yet for twenty-four hours and you've already got an invitation to a dinner party. The next thing we know, you'll be a debutante."

I reached for my orange juice. "Don't count on it."

"I'm sorry Fred couldn't have breakfast with us this morning."

"Where is Sir Frederic?" I asked.

"At the bank," Clark said. "Trying to get another business loan."

"For the Magic Mansion?"

Clark looked away. I followed his eyes to a calendar thumbtacked to the kitchen wall. Was there a deadline looming? "We're hopeful," he said.

"Is business that bad?" I asked.

He turned back and offered me a reassuring smile. "Everything will work out," he said, trying to convince us both. "It always does."

"Is there anything I can do?"

He pushed his plate of toast crumbs away. "Yes," he said. "Forget I even mentioned it and have a great time at the dinner party tonight."

I nodded. "Deal."

"Who did you say invited you?"

"Her name is Adrianna Marveaux."

Clark's eyes grew wide at first as if I'd said something that startled him. When he realized I was watching him, he shifted his focus and stared off in the distance as if trying to picture who she was. "That name sounds familiar."

"It does to me, too," I told him. "I swear I've heard it before."

"How is it that I don't know this woman?" he wondered aloud. "Avalon Cove is a really small place."

"I think she owns the boarding house," I explained. "The one on Lewis Lane."

He gave me a strange look. "Destiny, there's no boarding house on Lewis Lane. Or anywhere on the island, for that matter."

"At the very end of the block," I said.

"Are you talking about that old, decaying house?"

Uh-oh. He thinks you're insane. And, you probably are. Why can't you keep your ginormous mouth shut?

I looked at my fingernails. Maybe Tasha would loan me some of her pastel purple polish. "I think so," I said with a small shrug.

"I think that place is abandoned," Clark said. "No one's lived there for as long as I can remember. I'd stay away from there, if I were you. It could be dangerous. I don't want you to get hurt."

Clark's words hung in the air. I knew there was a hidden message floating in them somewhere. But why? What was he really trying to tell me? Did he know something about Wonderland?

I stood up and picked up my plate. "Maybe I wrote the address down wrong," I said. I moved toward the sink.

Clark sounded curious, a little suspicious, even. "Did you already go there?" he asked. "Did you go inside?"

I reached for the hot water knob. I didn't want to lie to Clark. I couldn't.

"Tasha and Topher…" I started to say. I stopped, hoping the right words would come to me.

The telephone on the kitchen wall rang. Clark stood up and reached for the receiver.

I exhaled a sigh of relief and concentrated on rinsing the rings of sticky maple syrup off my plate.

❖

I was standing next to Clark on the sidewalk, staring at a dark-haired mannequin in the front window of Bettina's. We were each holding to-go cups of peppermint tea, sipping occasionally. The hot liquid and the heavy humidity were making me sweat.

And it wasn't even ten o'clock in the morning yet.

Thankfully, I'd dressed more sensibly than I had yesterday. I was wearing a thin button-up blouse, shorts, and sandals. Still, the air was suffocating. Even with my hair up in a ponytail, it felt like a constant stream of sweat was sliding down my spine.

"That's it," Clark told me, tapping his index finger on the glass. I looked at him, noticing tiny beads of perspiration above his lip. He was hot in more than one way. My uncle was such a lucky guy. Clark was definitely out of his league. "That's the dress."

I nodded in agreement. It was a strapless cobalt blue vintage-style dress with a sweetheart neckline, with a poofy crinoline petticoat. It was straight out of one of those corny 50s movies about teenaged heartache. My grandmother adored Connie Francis and claimed to be her biggest fan. I knew she would've been proud. "What if it looks better on her than it does on me?" I worried, gesturing to the perfectly posed mannequin who looked at least two sizes smaller than me.

"Well," he said, slipping his arm through mine, "there's only one way to find out."

He led me into the air-conditioned boutique. High-energy dance music pumping out of huge overhead speakers assaulted our ears. I blinked, wanting the noise to go away. Was this a dress shop or a nightclub?

The place was cramped with overflowing racks of vintage clothes, purses, scarves, hats, sunglasses, and shoes, and what seemed like a mile-long display case of costume jewelry.

Incense smoke floated in the air, filling our lungs with the sweet and sticky smell of strawberries.

"Who's this?" a cigarette-strained voice half shouted over the raucous. I turned in the direction from which the voice had come.

"Wow," I heard myself say.

"Bettina, this is my…" Clark stopped. He looked at me, confused and cautious.

"I'm his illegitimate daughter," I said, just to see the reaction it provoked. His eyes widened. His cheeks paled. But the pink-haired, pierced, and tattooed Bettina curled her lips into a sneer I assumed was her attempt at a smile.

"Just kidding," I said with what I hoped was a Girl Scout grin and a giggle to match. "I'm his niece."

She flashed me a look of disappointment. "His niece, huh?" she said. "I liked it better when you were a love child."

"Me, too!" I answered, shouting to make myself heard. "And you must be the secret daughter of Joan Jett."

She sneered again, lifted her arm, and pointed a remote control at the sound system mounted on one of the walls. The music died. My ears were still ringing. "Nice try, kid," she said. "I'm Bettina. I own this place."

"I'm Destiny," I told her.

She took a step in my direction and said, "I know." Her eyes flicked up and down my body. She looked disgusted just by the sight of me. The expression of utter disdain on her face said I was either hideous or she'd caught a whiff of a sickening odor. Probably both. "You're…so…*blond*."

"Bettina," Clark said, sounding a bit nervous. "Destiny needs a dress."

Is he scared of her?

Bettina gave me another quick glance over with her frosty blue eyes. Her fake lashes reminded me of spider legs.

"You're not kidding," she assessed. "She needs a lot more than a dress."

"I already know what I want," I explained.

She raised a pierced eyebrow. "You sure about that, love child?"

I moved past them and stood facing the spine of the mannequin in the front window. "I want that," I said, my eyes fixed on the zipper of the dress.

Bettina was next to me before I'd realized she'd even moved. "Of course you do," she said into my ear. "It's his favorite color, isn't it?"

"What?" I stammered.

"Dominic," she said.

I felt my pulse quicken. Just the sound of his name sent a slight shudder through my body.

You're acting like an idiot, Destiny. You've haven't even met this guy. He could be hideous.

Yet, somehow I knew he wasn't.

And apparently so did Bettina. I turned, held her stare, and said, "Word must travel fast on this island."

When she spoke, I could feel her hot breath on my face. "I know everything that goes on in this town," she informed me. "Besides…some people say I have a gift."

I tried not to laugh. "Is that what you call it?" I asked. "What are you, the town psychic?"

She nodded, either missing my sarcasm or deciding to ignore it. "I give readings on the side. In case you ever need one," she said. "And you will."

"All I need is the dress," I insisted.

She put a hand on her hip. Her fingernails were painted black to match her lipstick. She wasn't very tall and she was too thin for her own good, but her presence was still a bit intimidating. She was older than me by at least ten years. I wondered if she had a little sister. Was *her* mother still alive? "For now it's just the dress," she said. "But you'll be back."

"Maybe," I said, glancing around the boutique. "This is a cool place."

"Yeah, Tasha and Topher think so, too."

"They didn't mention it."

"What time are they picking you up tonight?" she asked. "For the dinner party?"

"Were you invited?" I asked.

"I'm not welcome in that place." Her words were tinged with anger. "I tried once. I couldn't get the door to open."

"I guess that answers my question," I said.

"No," Bettina said, "I won't be there tonight."

"How can you claim to have a gift when you don't believe?" I asked.

She folded her arms across her chest and huffed, "Believe? In what?"

"Magic," I said, as if she knew.

"You can't put that on me."

"I'm right, aren't I?" I asked.

"Destiny, you're one to talk," she said. "We both know you don't believe in it either."

"Maybe I do now," I said.

"Magic isn't the same thing," she explained. "I believe in something different. For me, it's all about energy. It's about gravity. And you have more of it than you'll ever realize. *That's* why he'll be attracted to you. *That's* why Adrianna picked you. I'm sure of it." She looked over at Clark, who was mesmerized with something inside the glass display case. She lowered her voice a little. "What's going on in that house...that's bigger than anything I've ever encountered before. That's why I want in. To see it for myself."

"Who told you?" I asked. "About Wonderland?"

"People talk," she answered.

"It was either Tasha or Topher," I decided. "Or both. What'd you do, offer them free clothes in return?"

Bettina shot me a look. "Let me guess...you have a gift, too?"

"No."

"Then how'd you know?"

"Lucky guess."

I turned away from her. She stopped me by touching my arm. Static electricity caused a sharp and sudden shock between us. It jolted me.

"Ouch," I heard myself say.

"Is that the kind of girl you are?" she asked. "All magic and blond luck?"

"I'm just a girl who wants to buy a dress for a dinner party."

"Oh, yeah...the dress," she said. She reached for the zipper. The mannequin teetered and I wondered if it would fall over. Bettina steadied her and slipped the dress off the mannequin.

Bettina held the dress up in front of me. She tilted her head from side to side, as if she were trying to picture what I'd look like wearing it.

"I saw you in it already," she confessed. "I saw the entire dinner party. I have for over a week now."

If she was lying, she was doing a very convincing job.

"What did you see?" I asked, trying to keep my curiosity under control.

"You," she said. "Seconds before you see him for the first time. There's lots of flowers and little miniature cakes and teacups and twinkling lights. Like stars. They're everywhere. Shimmering." Bettina stopped to catch her breath. "But he's there. And the two of you...fall in love."

"Yeah, right," I said.

She touched my arm again. I looked into her eyes. "I already know what's going to happen to you."

I glanced across the store to make sure Clark was still occupied. "Tell me what you know," I said.

"About your mother?" she replied. "About the cancer?"

Bettina draped the dress over her arm and walked away. I felt stunned by her words, so it took me a second before I could move and follow her to a sky-blue slatted door covered with painted clouds.

"Wait...you knew my mother?" I asked.

Bettina opened the door, revealing a claustrophobic dressing room. She handed me the dress and gestured for me to step inside. I took a deep breath and did so. I heard the door click behind me. I was surrounded by mirrors. No matter what direction I turned, I could see myself.

I could hear Bettina's voice through the wall. "We went to high school together," she explained. "She was a senior. I was a freshman. We weren't exactly friends, but we knew each other. She was always dancing. I was busy dreaming about designing clothes."

I started to undress. "She never mentioned you before."

"Most people around here don't think I'm worth mentioning," Bettina said. "Except for the paranoid ones who think I'm trying to influence their daughters. I'm sure your Uncle Fred will warn you about me soon enough."

"No offense," I told her, slipping the dress on, "but you don't seem very dangerous."

"But you do," she answered.

I stared at my reflection and felt breathless. The dress fit perfectly. It was by the far the most incredible thing I'd ever worn. I looked like another person. Not me, but a version of me from the past. From another time, another era. Another life.

I also looked a lot like my mother.

"Me?" I said to my image in the smudged glass. "Dangerous? Hardly."

I turned the knob and pushed open the dressing room door.

I could see the approval in Bettina's heavily outlined eyes. She liked the way I looked in the dress.

"What's it like?" she asked. "Wonderland? Is it really how Tasha describes it?"

Over Bettina's shoulder, I could see Clark had lost interest in the costume jewelry. He'd moved on to a spinning rack of sunglasses. I hoped he was still out of earshot.

"It's too beautiful to talk about it," I explained. "I don't think words can do the place justice. Or Adrianna Marveaux, for that matter."

"Is she as beautiful as she is in her pictures?" Bettina asked.

"Yes," I said. "She's gorgeous. She'd probably love a lot of the clothes you have here, especially the vintage ones."

"Of course she would," Bettina boasted. "I sell glamour here. Or at least the illusion of it. And one thing's for certain, Adrianna Marveaux was a very glamorous woman. But I don't have to tell you that. It's obvious you take after her."

I found it difficult to breath. It was a wild combination of my fear of the unknown and the exhilaration I was discovering something that was so important, it would change my life.

"Take after her?" I repeated. "What do you mean?"

I couldn't remember where I'd put down my cup of peppermint tea, but my throat was so dry I needed some. I was finding it hard to swallow.

"You don't know?" Bettina asked. I shook my head. "You seriously have no idea?"

"I don't know anything about her," I said. "I swear."

Bettina peered into my eyes. "I believe you," she assessed. The rough edges around her words suddenly softened. "I know you're telling me the truth, Destiny. I can feel it."

"What am I missing, Bettina?" I askcd. "Please, tell me."

"Two very important pieces to this new crazy puzzle you've found yourself in," she said. "Adrianna Marveaux is no stranger to you."

"Have I met her before?"

"No. I don't think so," she said. "But you're related."

"How?" I asked.

"Adrianna Marveaux was your great-aunt. She was your grandfather's sister."

It took a few seconds for words to come out of my mouth. "I had no idea," I said. I wiped my forehead with the back of my hand. I felt dizzy. I needed to get out of the dress and back into my clothes. I needed to go. "Wait," I said, realizing. "You said *was*. You said she *was* my great aunt. As in past tense. But she still is. I just saw her yesterday. With my own eyes. I was in her house."

"I don't know how that's possible," Bettina said. "Unless… well…there's really only one way to explain it."

"Explain what?" I prompted, although a part of me already knew what Bettina was going to say, to reveal. "Tell me."

She took a breath, looked me in the eye, and said, "Adrianna Marveaux has been dead for over twelve years."

I heard a second voice coming from behind me, a familiar voice. It was tough and young. "I do," the female voice said. "I know how it's possible."

I turned. Tasha was standing in the doorway of the boutique.

She looked into my eyes and said with a grin, "It's magic."

CHAPTER FOUR

A seagull flying above let out a sharp cry before leaving us behind and gliding down toward the water's edge. The earsplitting noise the bird made was exactly the way I was feeling inside my head. I'd been wanting to scream out of sheer frustration and complete confusion since Tasha and I left Bettina's and walked the five blocks to the park in complete silence. I wanted answers but wasn't sure what questions I should be asking.

And even if I could figure that out, did anyone really know the answers I needed?

Tasha had taken charge of the scene at Bettina's. She instructed Clark to pay for the dress, take it home, and have it ready for me to wear in a few hours for what was now becoming the all-important dinner party. He agreed and didn't argue or protest when she explained to him that she needed to "borrow" me for an hour (possibly two) for some crucial "girl talk." Then, very politely, Tasha cautioned a very curious Bettina to leave me alone, and as she'd put it in a gentle whisper, "Find something better to do than harass a fifteen-year-old girl whose mother has just died."

"Get me an invite to Wonderland and I'll do whatever you ask," Bettina replied.

Smug and in control, Tasha replied, "You already do."

Tasha was now sitting in a swing on the playground. Her hands were wrapped around the silver links of the chain ropes that held the swing midair above the sand. The sunlight made her purple nail polish seem even brighter.

She hadn't looked at me since we'd arrived ten minutes ago. Was she trying to find the right words to tell me I wasn't completely insane? That somehow my great-aunt was a whacked-out matchmaking ghost living in and haunting an old house?

I was sitting nearby on the cold metal edge of the slide. We had the entire playground to ourselves. Without any children around, the place seemed creepy and quiet.

I couldn't take the silence anymore.

I cleared my throat. I folded my arms across my chest. I looked at Tasha. "Is it true?" I asked. "Am I really related to her?"

Tasha nodded. "Yes. That's what she says."

"And she's dead?"

Tasha's thick yellow headband was sliding down into her feline shaped eyes. She pushed it back into place with her index finger and said, "That's what everyone tells me. Topher and me did some research. We went to the library and looked through old newspapers and stuff like that. We found Adrianna's obituary. It mentions you. And your mom."

"Please explain this to me," I said. "I know we don't know each other very well, Tasha, but I'm really freaked out by everything I've experienced in the last twenty-four hours. Nothing makes any sense in this place. And all I want to do right now is get on the first plane back to Chicago. My life was normal there."

She looked at me then and asked, "Destiny, why are you scared?"

"I'm not," I answered, but we both knew I was lying. "I just want you to convince me that I'm not crazy."

"Maybe you are," she said. "Maybe we all are. How am I supposed to know? I'm not an expert on *everything*."

I stood up and walked across the playground. Grains of sand sifted between my toes, sliding between the bottoms of my feet and the soles of my sandals. It felt like I was walking on a thin layer of sandpaper. I circled back and sat down in the empty swing next to Tasha and kicked off my shoes.

"Did I imagine everything that happened to me at Wonderland?" I asked. "Was it real? I mean, does that place even exist? Or did you or Topher slip me something?"

"Why would we do something like that?" she asked. I could tell my accusation had made her angry.

I made a point of softening my tone. "You didn't answer my question."

"No," she stated firmly. "We didn't. If you don't believe me, you can ask Topher yourself." She gestured with a slight jerk of her head in the direction of town. I peered into the distance and saw Topher approaching on foot, fast.

"They're chasing him again?" I said.

Tasha stepped out of the swing. "You know the drill," she told me.

I grabbed my sandals and moved quickly to the cement tunnel in the center of the playground. Barefoot, I knelt down and crawled inside. Within seconds, Topher dove in next to me, from the opposite end. He scrambled toward me, grabbed my hand, and squeezed it so hard it hurt. "They almost got me," he gasped.

He was breathing so fast, I was worried he might hyperventilate and pass out. His chest pulsed and throbbed like something was inside it, kicking and fighting to escape. I watched the front of his black T-shirt rise and fall, feeling hypnotized by the rapid movement. A bead of sweat trickled down the side of his soft face.

He looked at me and I felt an immense sense of sadness. His blue-gray eyes were filled with tears. I could tell he was trying not to cry.

"You're okay now," I whispered.

He shook his head. He wiped his eyes with the back of his trembling hand, smearing black guyliner across his cheek.

Outside, I could hear Tasha defending her best friend. Her no-nonsense voice was tough and commanding. She was clearly in charge of the situation and calling the shots on the playground.

I was afraid. Had Topher been spotted? Did they know he was hiding just a few feet away from where they stood? What would they do to him if they found him? I felt the need to protect him, stick up for him and defend him. But if they attacked him, what would I be able to do? Sure, I was tall, but as Samantha had always said, "You have a big mouth, Destiny, but we both know you can't back it up."

It was true. I was definitely no fighter.

"Don't you guys have anything else better to do, Nathan?" Tasha asked. "Aren't there some desperate new freshman girls you can impress?"

"Where is he?" a guy's voice asked. It was light and airy and drenched with a Southern twang. Topher tightened his grip on my hand just at the sound of it.

"We ain't gonna hurt him," said another guy with a much deeper voice and identical accent.

"Yeah," a third voice agreed. His voice sounded cold and cruel. There was a permanent mean streak in him, and it echoed in every slow syllable he spoke. "We just wanna talk to him for a few minutes."

"That's not gonna happen," Tasha replied. "Not today.

And not ever. If it did, well…then I'd have to tell *your* mom about the time you snuck her car out of the garage and hit that stop sign. Isn't filing a police report for a car that wasn't *really* stolen a felony of some sort?" She took a breath before moving on to the next jerk. "And I'd have to tell Leslie all about how you tried to make out with her best friend after Homecoming last year. Think she won't believe me, Skeeter? Maybe she'll love my cell phone as much as I do. It takes awesome pictures." I could almost hear the smirk in her voice. She hated these guys. Then again, who could blame her? They were total jerks. "And *you*—if you even *think* about touching him, Boyd, I'll tell the entire school you gave me an STD."

"You're bluffing," the icy one challenged.

"Try me," she said. "I dare you."

"You think you can just blackmail us?" the one with the deep voice asked.

"*Black*mail?" she repeated. "Is that some sort of racist remark? Do I need to call my cousins in Atlanta to come up here?"

I had to cover my mouth with my hand to hold back my laughter. Did these guys even realize how dumb they were?

Tasha apparently knew.

"We don't got a problem with you, Tasha."

"And Topher doesn't have a problem with any of you," she replied. "Yet the three of you chase him down like a dog every day and I have no idea why. Don't you have jobs or like to play basketball or have girlfriends? I mean, is this really all you have to do with your time? This is how you wanna spend the last few weeks of summer?"

They were quiet for a moment. Finally one of them answered her with a simple "Yeah."

"We won't be happy until we catch him," said the one with the evil-sounding voice.

"You think beating him to a pulp is gonna make him like girls?" she asked.

"Yeah."

"Maybe."

"We don't know. But it's worth a try."

"Topher *does* like girls," she said. "He adores them. He respects them, too. He's just different than the three of you."

"Yeah, 'cause he's a freak."

"Go home or I kick my plan into action," Tasha said, exasperated. "I'm not kidding. I have nothing to lose by destroying your pathetic lives."

They were quiet. Were they challenging her? Trying to figure out just how far Tasha would go? I knew she wouldn't back down.

"Who are you calling?" one of them asked.

"Hi," she said into what I assumed was her cell phone. "Is Leslie there? It's Tasha. From school."

"Hang up the phone!"

"Okay, okay," one of them said. "You win! We give up."

"That's okay," she said to the person on the other end. "Just let her know I'll try calling her again later. Thanks. Bye."

"You win, Tasha—for now," said the one with the deep voice.

"Lucky break for all of us, I guess," she said. "Now disappear before I change my mind. Nothing would make me happier than to see the three of you suffer."

"Just remember," the evil one, apparently the redneck ringleader, said to her, "summer ain't over yet."

Seconds later, Tasha appeared in one of the open ends of the cement tunnel, kneeling beside me. She pushed her yellow headband out of her brown eyes again, wiped her palms clean of sand, and said to us, "I hope the two of you aren't planning to go to the dinner party looking like that."

I crawled over Topher and slid out of the tunnel on the opposite end. I stood up and so did Tasha. Our eyes locked over the top of the cement cylinder. Topher stayed inside his place of refuge.

"I don't think I'm going at all," I said.

Tasha sighed, placed a hand on her hip, and gave me a look of sheer disbelief. "Are you kidding me?"

"I don't understand any of it," I explained. "And neither one of you wants to fill me in."

Topher suddenly popped up. "We can't," he offered.

"It has to do with love," Tasha added. "Tonight, you'll understand everything, Destiny. I promise. Adrianna picked you. She said she picked all three of us."

"Pick someone else," I threw back at her. "I'm not interested."

I turned and started to walk away. I was surprised when they followed me. Within seconds, the three of us were moving shoulder to shoulder. I walked faster as we left the park. I had no idea where I was going, but I couldn't stop walking. I was angry. Confused. Frustrated.

"I know this entire situation seems really crazy," Topher said.

"She wouldn't have picked you without a reason," Tasha echoed.

"She said there had to be three of us," Topher insisted. "Hope...faith..."

"But the greatest of these is—" Tasha began.

I stopped in my tracks and finished her thought with "Love."

I looked at my two new friends. They were breathless.

Their foreheads were covered with thin layers of sweat. But there was genuine concern in their eyes. They didn't know me very well, but it was evident they really did care.

Damn it, why do they have to be so nice to me? It would be so much easier just to walk away if they were total jerks.

I thought about leaving them there, standing on the sidewalk in the middle of town. Maybe I'd go back to my new home and ask Clark to help me get ready. Or I'd find the Magic Mansion and ask Sir Frederic the Great for some advice on what to do. Or I could hitchhike to the airport, call Samantha, have her wire me some money, and fly back to Chicago where I belonged.

"You have to understand where I'm coming from," I said.

"We're trying to," Topher said. "Honest."

"Here," Tasha said, ushering me gently over to a green wrought-iron café table and chairs on the sidewalk outside a corner coffee shop. "Let's all sit and talk this out."

"You sound like a camp counselor," I said, trying not to smile.

"In another life, maybe," she replied. "In this one, I wanna be a comic book hero. Or the lead singer of an all-girl punk band. Or a Japanese pop star."

I relented and sat down. The smooth edge of the metal chair chilled the back of my knees, much like the slide had when Tasha and I were sitting in the playground just minutes ago.

"Better?" Tasha asked.

I nodded in reply.

"Let me get you something to drink," she offered, reaching into the front pocket of her jeans.

"Fine," I agreed. "But no more peppermint tea. I love the stuff, but it's way too hot to drink that here."

"Fruit smoothie?" she suggested.

I nodded. "Only if it's chocolate and banana," I sang.

"That's not a smoothie, Destiny. That's a shake," she informed me. I gave her a look. "Okay, okay. I'll see what I can work out." She disappeared into the shop.

I glanced up at the flag of Ireland, attached to a white plastic flagpole poking out of the stony arched entryway. The green, white, and orange striped fabric was rippling and waving above us, but I felt no breeze.

A few tables away a man who looked like Santa Claus was smoking a pipe and reading a newspaper. The smell of the tobacco made me think of my grandfather, the eccentric magician. I had only one memory of him. I was five. He'd lifted me up above his head, laughing. He brought me down to eye level, kissed both of my cheeks, and whispered in my ear, "I love you, little one." I remembered his rough skin smelling like sweet tobacco. Just like the smoke billowing out of the stranger's pipe.

"You okay?" Topher asked from where he sat across from me.

"I will be," I said. "Just as soon as I get some answers."

A few women wearing expensive-looking sunglasses strolled past us, clutching shopping bags and cups of coffee. I stared at them, wondering if I'd ever be that glamorous, that sophisticated. But did I even want to be? They seemed aloof and cold. No matter how hard I tried, I could never pretend to not care.

"I used to be like you," Topher said, almost like he was reading my mind. "In the beginning, when I first went to Wonderland. I didn't understand it. I thought it was a dream."

"Is it?" I asked. "Because that's the only way to explain it that makes any kind of sense to me."

"I wish I could tell you everything you wanna hear, Destiny," he said.

I believed him. "I don't know if I wanna go back there," I confessed.

"I felt the same way," he said. "But now, I don't regret it."

To me, Topher looked like a rock star sitting there in the sun in front of the Irish café. He was the epitome of cool. He was sexy and sensitive. His jagged, jet-black hair and smudged guy-liner only added to his unique look.

He should be onstage standing behind a microphone, singing about what it's like living with a broken heart.

"Have you ever been in love before?" I asked.

He seemed surprised by the question. His pale cheeks turned a light shade of pink. "No...I don't know," he stammered, lowering his eyes, which were the color of a stormy sky. "I mean...I've had crushes before."

"Yeah, me, too," I said.

"But I've never even kissed a guy," he admitted.

"Never?" I said. "Not even when you were a kid?"

"Not even during the endless games of Truth or Dare Tasha used to make us all play."

"You'll meet the right person," I assured him. "We all will."

"That's what Adrianna says," he told me. "That's what tonight is for all of us. A chance to come face-to-face with our true love. Tasha and Juliet. Me and Pablo. And you and Dominic. We've never met them before, but Adrianna told us about them. How they want to meet us."

I sat up in my chair, alert. "Wait...the dinner party?" I said. "It's a triple date?"

Topher nodded. "Why else do you think me and Tasha are so nervous?"

I smiled at Topher. "I don't know you guys well enough yet to be able to tell."

"Don't be fooled by her," he said. "Tasha might seem like she's in control on the outside, but really she's a hot mess."

I sighed, relieved. "So am I."

"Yeah," Topher agreed, "but with you it's a lot easier to tell."

"Am I that obvious?" I asked.

"You don't like this place very much, do you?"

"Avalon Cove?" I said. "Or this coffee shop?"

Tasha suddenly appeared with bottles of water tucked under each arm and a filled-to-the-brim frosty mug in her hand. "As the lady requested," she said. "A chocolate and banana shake." She put the delicious-looking drink down in front of me and handed me a paper-covered straw.

"I'd feel a lot less guilty about drinking it if we agreed to call it a smoothie," I told her, unwrapping the straw.

She looked down at me and our eyes met. "Promise me you'll go back to Wonderland tonight and we can call it whatever you want," she said.

I reached for the straw, prepared to take my first sip.

I glanced up at Tasha and smiled. "Deal."

❖

A few hours later, I was dressed and ready to go. After one final inspection in the mirror in my bathroom, I teetered from my pink bedroom in a pair of white heels I hadn't worn in over a year. I started to make my way down the stairs, clutching the banister for dear life.

With my luck, I was worried I'd slip, fall down the stairs, break every bone in my body, and spend the rest of the summer in a body cast.

Halfway down the staircase, I heard the faint sound of the *Wheel of Fortune* theme music. I knew Tasha and Topher would be arriving at any second to pick me up, but I wanted to get one last nod of approval on my dress from Uncle Fred and Clark. Especially from Clark, since my Uncle Fred spent most of his life in a cape, top hat, tuxedo shirt, and black slacks, waving a glitter-tipped magic wand around. In this family, Clark was clearly my only resource for decent fashion advice. Also, we had yet to discuss a curfew, so I was hoping to get that nailed down once and for all.

Something I heard caused me to freeze on the second to the last step.

"We've got bigger problems than that," I heard Clark say. There was a layer of panic in his tone that made me feel nervous. Like I was hearing something I wasn't supposed to.

I felt a strange nervous energy start to tickle somewhere inside my body. I was grateful the TV volume was low. Otherwise, I'd never be able to listen to their conversation.

"What could be worse than losing the Magic Mansion?" Uncle Fred replied. "I can't change their minds. I can't force them to give us another loan. The bank has all the power."

Damn. They really are losing the business. After all these years. My grandfather's heart is probably breaking in heaven. Maybe my mother is there with him.

"I'm not talking about bank loans," Clark said. "I'm talking about Destiny."

Me? What did I do?

"Did she do something wrong?" my Uncle Fred asked.

Did I? It's only my second day here. How much damage could I have caused in such a short time?

"No," Clark said. "She's a sweet kid. I'm thrilled she's here. And I know you are, too. In fact, I haven't seen you this happy in years."

"You know I've always wanted children," Uncle Fred reminded Clark.

"Well, maybe we should be careful what we wish for."

"Hon, if you're about to tell me you're pregnant, let me call the bank first. I'll tell them we don't need their stinking loan, because we'll be filthy rich."

"Fred, I'm being serious," Clark said.

"I know," he said. "I'm just not sure why."

Clark was quiet for a second before he spoke. Then, "I think she knows."

I felt dizzy. My palms started to sweat. I wanted to run.

"What are you talking about?" Uncle Fred asked. "What does she know?"

"She mentioned her name this morning. At breakfast."

"Who?"

"Adrianna Marveaux," Clark whispered. "She said she met her."

"Dear God…how?"

"How do you think?" Clark said. "She went to Wonderland."

"No. That's not possible. She's been here for two days. No one even knows about that place."

"Not true," Clark said. "We do."

"Are you sure? Maybe you made a mistake or she—"

"I'm positive. That's who invited her to the party tonight. She's having dinner with Adrianna. She's going back to Wonderland. So you know what that means."

"She was chosen," my uncle said. "Of course she was. It makes sense, Clark. Think about it."

"But what if she figures it out?" Clark sounded almost terrified. "Will something happen to us? Will it change everything?"

"I don't know," my uncle said.

"It's not like we can go back to Wonderland to ask her ourselves."

"Then we don't have a choice," Uncle Fred decided.

"You think we should just sit around and wait? Fred, how can we?"

"Simple. We go on. Life as usual."

"It'll drive us crazy. I'll be worried constantly. She's a smart girl. She's gonna figure it out."

"Then let's pray she doesn't." For a moment, I thought Uncle Fred was going to cry. His voice cracked with a flood of emotion. "I can't lose you again."

I have to get out of here. I've heard too much.

To make my presence known, I made loud footsteps on the stairs, nearly stomping. Within moments they both appeared at the bottom of the staircase, smiling.

"You look gorgeous," my uncle said, beaming.

I stared into his bloodshot eyes and asked, "Uncle Fred, what's the matter? Have you been crying?"

"No, silly," he said. "Just a bad case of allergies."

"He's allergic to everything," Clark added.

"Especially to Alex Trebek," my uncle joked.

My eyes shifted back and forth between them. Could they tell I'd been listening on the stairs? Did they suspect me? I thought about telling them I'd heard their entire conversation. And in return, I wanted them to tell me everything.

Instead I asked, "What time should I be home?"

They exchanged a look. It was clearly their first executive decisions as parents.

"By midnight," Uncle Fred decided. Clark nodded his agreement.

I leaned in and kissed my uncle's cheek. "I'll be home before the clock strikes twelve," I promised. "Don't wait up."

"Don't fool yourself," Clark told me. "He won't be able to sleep until he knows you're safe."

I stopped at the front door and looked back at them.

"You guys are sweet," I said. "Thank you for letting me live here."

"You're family," my uncle said.

"This is your home," Clark agreed.

"We're happy you're here with us," Uncle Fred added.

I looked at them for a moment, studying their faces. Even though they were smiling at me, I could still see a hint of fear in their eyes.

They had a secret. And for some reason, they were frightened I was going to discover what it was.

Something inside told me the answer to all of my questions would be found at Wonderland.

"Thank you," I said to them. I opened the front door and stepped outside. The night air was heavy and rich with a sweet, flowery smell.

Tasha was parked at the curb in a beat-up old pickup truck. Topher was leaning out the passenger window, smiling and waving at me.

"Nothing like traveling in style," I said once I reached the faded golden truck. I opened the door. Topher slid over to make room for me. He looked very handsome in a burgundy velvet blazer, black and white striped button-up shirt, pleated black slacks, and shiny black dress shoes.

Tasha was wearing a peach-colored halter dress. It looked so soft I was tempted to reach across Topher just to touch it.

"Don't judge me," Tasha said. "My only other choice of transportation was my old skateboard."

"Who drives this thing?" I asked, reaching for the seat belt.

"I have no idea," she said. "We stole it."

"Seriously?" I panicked.

"No," she said, "but it was so worth it just to see that look on your face. It belongs to my stepfather. He owns a landscaping business. I had to beg him to let us borrow it."

"That explains the lawn mower in the back," I said. "Don't mess with me tonight. Either one of you. I'm feeling kind of fragile right now."

"What's the issue?" Tasha asked, pulling away from my house. "I can tell something's wrong."

"I just overheard a really weird conversation between my uncle and his husband."

"Care to share?" she said. "Topher and me know pretty much everything about everyone around here."

"I think they've been to Wonderland before."

"They have," Topher confirmed. He smelled good—I couldn't quite place his cologne.

"Yeah," Tasha added. "How else do you think we found out about it?"

"Are you lying to me again?" I asked.

"No," Tasha promised. "I swear."

"They took the two of you to Wonderland?" I asked.

"No." Topher shook his head. "We followed your uncle there."

CHAPTER FIVE

Who are you?" My question floated in the golden air. My voice cut through the brilliant rays of light streaming down from somewhere above, filling the space between us with light. The beams were thick before dissolving into warm patches and pools on the wooden floor of the old house. I wanted to step into one of the shafts of light just to feel its soft and gentle burn on my skin.

Adrianna held my stare. She smiled at me with her striking green eyes. "You know who I am," she replied. "And it's true. I am your great-aunt."

I was standing in the foyer, still a little jittery from the adrenaline rush from arriving in Wonderland. I struggled to catch my breath. I looked around for Tasha and Topher. They'd been with me just seconds ago. The three of us had held each other's hands spiraling through the warm, comforting dark. Into another dimension. Maybe even another world.

But when I opened my eyes, my friends were already gone.

Adrianna was posed on the last step of the staircase, wearing a pale green tulle party dress. The soft, almost pastel color matched the shade of her haunting eyes perfectly. The pleated bodice was trimmed with tiny jewels. They sparkled without her even moving, shooting wild patterns of reflected light all around us. She glittered in the warm dim glow of the chandelier above. Her platinum hair hung loosely in large curls around her face, spilling down to her bare shoulders. She looked like a Greek goddess, a modern-day version of Aphrodite.

Or a fairy godmother in training.

Just seconds ago I was standing in front of the massive house, blown away by the complete transformation. I couldn't believe my eyes. I climbed out of the beat-up pickup truck, stood on the sidewalk, and gaped in awe at the beautiful sight before me.

Something wonderful had happened to the decrepit house. The Victorian architecture was still the same, including the castle-like tower, but now it evoked a stunning allure, welcoming rather than repelling. It radiated from within with an inviting luminosity. The landscaping surrounding the estate was exquisite. I'd never seen so many white roses and red tulips. It was a vision of lush and romantic grandeur.

"What happened?" I asked Tasha and Topher.

"What do you mean?" Topher replied.

"This place…it looks completely different," I said, still staring in disbelief. "How is this possible? We were just here yesterday."

Tasha laughed a little. "Once you've been inside Wonderland, it never looks the same again," she explained.

"You're able to see the magic now," Topher added. "Just like us."

Arm in arm we walked through rays of silvery moonlight to the wooden front steps and up to the freshly painted porch. We rang the melodic doorbell and waited with anticipation.

Now Adrianna and I were standing face-to-face in the foyer. She was giving me an inquisitive look, like she knew I had more questions to ask.

"None of this is real, is it?" I said. "All of this is in my imagination."

"On the contrary," she replied. "This is very real."

"It can't be," I insisted.

"Why not?" she asked.

I stared at her skin, her flawless, smooth complexion. She was like a painting that had come to life. Or, in her case, back from the dead. "People say you died over twelve years ago."

She offered me a gentle smile. "Death is a tricky thing," she said. "It's very complicated."

"Much like life?"

"You seem frustrated, Destiny," she decided. "Have I upset you in some way?"

"I'm scared that I'm crazy," I explained. "Have I gone completely insane?"

"I can assure you," she said, "your sanity is perfectly intact."

"Maybe this is my fault," I wondered aloud. "Maybe because of what happened to my mother, I've snapped somehow and this is my way of dealing with it. Before my mom got sick, I was just a normal girl in Chicago."

"Without a care in the world?" she asked.

"Something like that," I agreed. "None of this makes sense."

"You're looking for an explanation," she said with a nod.

"Yes," I said. "Why am I here?"

Adrianna came down the last step. She moved toward me in a smooth, gliding manner. She reached out her hands and covered mine. Her palms and fingertips felt like spun silk. She looked deep into my eyes. "Because I chose you," she said.

"But why?" I persisted. "There's nothing special about me."

She gave me a look of confusion. "You couldn't be more wrong."

Adrianna turned away and moved quickly through the house. I followed the scent of her powerful perfume into the library. She was lying across the red velvet chaise, curled up next to a very sleepy Montgomery. I sat across from them in the plush gold velvet love seat. My vintage-style dress flared out in a circle of cobalt blue and crinoline.

Adrianna cleared her throat, as if to command my attention.

Is it my imagination, or did the room just get darker?

"You have a choice to make, Destiny," she said. "It's important, and you must make it now. Otherwise, I will have to ask you to leave Wonderland and never come back."

I swallowed. "Ask me," I said.

She rested an elbow on the arm of the chaise lounge. Every movement she made was slow and graceful. Like liquid. "Do you believe in true love?"

I glanced away. The floor-to-ceiling walls of books had momentarily distracted me. I wanted to read them all. I wanted to spend the next week inside this room, devouring every book I could get my hands on and drinking endless pots of tea. I wanted to listen to Beethoven on the phonograph and imagine ballroom dancing with heroes and princes who would spring to life from the pages of a classic novel. I wanted to take a catnap next to Montgomery, bask in the constant puddles of sunlight, and dream my parents were still married and I was an only child. I wanted Adrianna to like me. I wanted her to tell me about my past. My ancestors. Family secrets.

I want to see my mother again.

"I don't know," I answered.

"Answer the question," she said.

"I did."

"I'll ask it again. You have to be certain. There's no room for hesitation. Do you believe in love, Destiny? Something worth dying for? Do you believe it's possible that two people are meant for each other?"

"You're asking me if I believe in forever, but I'm only fifteen," I reminded her. "I can't even drive yet. How am I supposed to know if true love exists?"

"What does your heart say?" she pushed. "Never mind what others have told you."

An image of my mother and father floated into my mind. I was in the backseat of our old car, drifting off to sleep as most six-year-olds do during a long car ride. It was nighttime. There was a light rain tiptoeing across the windshield. My mother was in the passenger seat. I saw her face, her profile, when she turned and looked at my father. She didn't say a word. She didn't touch him. She didn't have to. I knew from the love in her eyes everything she was feeling in that moment.

"Yes," I said. "I believe."

She nodded. "I know. I just needed to hear you say it."

I licked my lips. I suddenly felt very thirsty. "Is that why you brought me here?"

"When the time is right, how things work at Wonderland will be explained to you," she said. "Everything you want to know will be revealed. Even the questions you're too afraid to ask."

"You won't tell me tonight?" I asked.

She shook her head. "I'll know when you're ready," she said. "So will you."

I looked at the books again and back to a sleepy-eyed Montgomery. I focused on my beautiful great-aunt sitting like a platinum-haired version of Cleopatra on her velvet throne.

"I've never been in love before," I confessed. "For some reason…guys don't pay very much attention to me."

"Perhaps you haven't met the right gentleman yet," she suggested.

"Is he here?" I asked. "Dominic?" It was the first time I'd said his name. The word felt natural for me to say. Like I'd been saying it all my life. Like it belonged to me.

"Yes," she said with a sly smile. "He's been waiting for you since he arrived last month. You're his dance partner tonight. You're the guest of honor."

"Did you bring me here just so I could meet him?" I asked.

Now it was her turn to look away. "You could say that," she replied.

"Why are you being so vague?"

She met my eyes from across the coffee table. "You're here for many reasons, Destiny. Very few people are invited to Wonderland. You'll come to learn this is a very special place. And it takes an exceptional person to believe in it. Wonderland can't exist without it. You have to have certainty in your heart. Doubt and fear will destroy this place. Love and magic is what makes Wonderland happen."

"Magic," I repeated. "Everyone keeps asking me if I believe in it. Ever since I got to Avalon Cove."

"I already know your answer," she said. "You are my brother's only granddaughter. He always knew you believed in magic. Even if you didn't know it for yourself."

"Is that what this is?" I asked. "Is Wonderland just one big magic trick? Am I stuck in an optical illusion?"

"You're in the center of many hearts," she said. "Some find their way here on their own. Some have to be shown the way. Others are lost until they get here."

"And me?" I asked. "Was I lost?"

She straightened her posture. "Never," she replied.

"I wish I would've known you," I said. "I mean, when I was younger."

She shook her head. "I would've been of no use to you then. I died when you were three."

"But we're related," I said. "We're family."

"Yes, we are," she said. "But we both know family isn't always biological."

"Are you talking about Clark and my Uncle Fred?" I asked. "They're a family."

"Absolutely," she agreed. "And what of Tasha and Topher? In a very short time, they've come to mean a lot to each other. And to you."

"I like them," I said. "But I don't know them very well."

Adrianna leaned forward a little. There was concern in her voice. "I'm worried about Topher."

"I thought everything was perfect here," I said. "It seems like there are no worries in Wonderland."

"Here he is safe," she assured me. "We all are. But he can't stay here forever. In fact, he's already running out of time. It's the outside world that concerns me. It's a very cruel place for a boy like Topher."

The fear on her face told me the answer to my question, but I asked it anyway. "Because he's gay?"

"He's tormented every day by those young men."

"They're idiots," I said.

"That's easy for you and me to say," she said. "Imagine what they are to Topher."

"Monsters," I said. "He probably feels like he's living in a nightmare."

"Just because he's different," she said. "Because he's

brave enough to love. For that he should be persecuted and punished?"

"He has Tasha," I reminded her. "And me."

"Does he?"

"I know Tasha protects him. And my uncles treat him like family. Or so he says."

"Everything will change for Topher after tonight," she said.

I gave her a look. "What do you mean? For the better? Or for the worse?"

"That's still to be determined. I'm giving him a chance at true love," she explained. "It's a gift I'm giving to each of you."

I folded my arms across my chest. "So you're a matchmaker?"

"In conventional terms, yes. But Topher has the greatest risk. It won't be as easy for him to love as it will be for you or Tasha. The men in your world give greater permission to women."

"I'm not sure why you're telling me this."

"Because he's going to need you," she said. "They both will. And you're going to need them."

"Is that why we met?"

"Everything happens for a reason," she said. "Don't you agree?"

"So far it seems that way," I said. "So my mother had to die in order for me to come to Avalon Cove so I could meet Tasha and Topher and they could bring me to Wonderland… to you?"

"The reason you're here is much more complex than that," she said. "It's bigger than you."

"I'm here because of love?"

Adrianna swung her legs over the edge of the chaise. I watched as her transparent Cinderella-like high heels touched the wooden floor. She stood, reached for me with both hands, and breathed with an infectious urgency, "It's time. It's now."

I hurried to my feet, quickened by the anxiousness in her eyes. "What? What do you mean?"

"He's ready," she decided. "You both are."

"How can you tell?"

"Ask questions later. You don't get very much time with him. I don't want to waste a second."

"I don't understand."

"Follow me," she instructed. I did as I was told. We left the library and moved through a maze of hallways. I felt dizzy and disoriented, like I was trapped in an endless corridor full of sharp twists and turns. There were sconces on the walls with flame-shaped lightbulbs in them. They pulsed and flickered like genuine candlelight, but I knew they were artificial. The effect cast our moving shadows on the surfaces around us, splashing our figures across the gold and cream-colored striped wallpaper.

The haphazard hallway ended, opening up into a beautiful old-fashioned kitchen bathed in blue and silver strips of moonlight pouring in through an open window above the porcelain sink. White lace curtains trimmed with embroidered patterns of pastel greens, pinks, blues, and yellows billowed and fluttered from a cool night breeze tumbling inside from the open space between the sill and the wooden frame of the window. At once, the refreshing air clung to my skin, bringing me a sense of relief and calm.

Then I saw him. I stopped in my tracks. He was an old man sitting at the kitchen table in a red vinyl-covered chair. He was bent over a game of solitaire. He held a card in one hand—the queen of hearts. He had a head of thick gray and black disheveled hair. My eyes drifted down to his bony knuckles, his wrinkled and splotched skin. He looked up. Our eyes met. It seemed as if he knew me because his mouth lifted into a warm, welcoming smile.

"Destiny," he said.

Adrianna touched my arm, jolting me back to the task at hand. "There isn't time for him right now," she said. "I don't want you to be late. You only get one dance with Dominic."

"Who is he?" I asked Adrianna. When she didn't respond, I turned to him. "Do I know you?"

The old man continued to smile at me in response. I fought with the urge to go to him and embrace him. There was a kindness in his eyes I'd never seen before.

"He never got the chance to meet you," my great-aunt said. "He's my husband. He's Alfred. He died before you were born."

"She looks like her mother," he said. "Like an angel."

"You know better," she reprimanded him gently. "We never use that word in Wonderland."

"My apologies, my queen," he said. His attention returned to his card game.

Adrianna led me to a wooden door in the far corner of the moonlit kitchen. Was she sending me down to a basement? Outside to a backyard? "Are you ready?" she asked.

"You would know that answer better than me," I replied.

"What you're about to experience is something most have never had the chance to. Only a select few have ever made it this far in Wonderland."

"I'm one of the lucky ones?"

"No," she said. "This has nothing to do with luck. You're here because you believe in love."

"And magic," I reminded her.

"Once I open this door and you cross the threshold, you need to know...there's no turning back, Destiny."

I nodded. "I understand."

"You're going to be faced with the most difficult choice of your life. Even the choices that are still to come in your future—none of them will compare to this one, do you understand?"

"What am I choosing?" I asked.

I watched her hand move to the shiny brass door knob. Her fingers wrapped around it. She turned it slowly. "Between life and death," she answered.

She pulled the door open. The hinges creaked with a loud groan. I saw nothing in front of me except never-ending darkness. "You don't have much time," she explained. "Make the most of it while you can."

I looked into my great-aunt's eyes. "I'm not afraid," I assured her.

She leaned in and kissed my cheek. "I know," she said. I felt her palm on the middle of my back, guiding me gently toward the sea of black. "Some answers you will find inside," she explained. "The others will be given to you when you return."

I took a step forward. The door closed behind me. My entire body began to tremble. An intense sensation took my breath away. I felt something or someone wrap around my body and pull me forward with great speed. It was the same thrill as the first big dip on a roller-coaster ride. I was flying in the air. I could feel the wind against my ears. Then my body was tilted forward. I began to free fall, face first. Soaring through nothing but darkness, I felt euphoric.

I gave in to the impulse to shut my eyes. That's when I

landed. My body collided with something soft and delicate. Pillows? Clouds? A giant mattress?

I opened my eyes. I was on my back. The first things I saw were Chinese paper lanterns. There were hundreds of them, clinging to silver wires crisscrossing above me. Each lantern was illuminated from within, casting a warm glow. No two lanterns were the same color. A few of them swayed in the gentle breeze, gliding from side to side with a rhythm all their own. The sight of them was stunning. I watched them with an almost trance-like intensity, mesmerized by the beauty of their light and the colors they emitted.

Instinct kicked in and reminded me I was somewhere new and unfamiliar. I stood up quickly and turned in slow circles to take in everything surrounding me. My high heels sank into the soft earth. I glanced down expecting to see grass or dirt. The entire surface was covered with what looked to be tiny shards of multicolored broken glass. It was if someone had split open a million kaleidoscopes and scattered their contents all over the ground beneath my feet.

I was standing in the middle of a garden of sorts. Or was it a courtyard? It was a square plot of land, surrounded on all four sides by ivy-colored gray stone walls. There was no entrance. There was no way out. Unless I wanted to scale my way up toward the star-filled sky and tiptoe across constellations.

I didn't feel threatened or in danger. In fact, I felt quite the opposite. A tickle of invincibility began to stir inside me. Within seconds, I felt convinced anything was possible. It was a swell of confidence mixing wildly with an electric burst of optimism. I had no doubt. No fear. No worries.

I never wanted to leave.

I was surrounded by more flowers than I could count— every type, every color, and every scent. It was intoxicating. I leaned in toward a row of white carnations. I inhaled deeply, weakened by their sweet fragrance. I realized then that it was difficult for me to breathe. I placed my hand across my chest. My heartbeat vibrated against my skin.

You're okay. Just breathe.

"Don't worry," a familiar voice said. I turned and smiled when I saw Tasha standing beside me in her peach-colored halter dress. She was holding a bouquet of wildflowers. "I've been here for a few minutes. It gets easier to breathe in a moment or two."

Tasha was right. Almost at once, I felt at ease. A sudden calm washed over me, and any lingering apprehension dissipated. My shoulders relaxed. My body felt light. The euphoria continued to surge through me.

"I've never felt like this before," I confessed.

"Me either," she said.

"It's like…" I stopped, searching for the words. "Absolute bliss."

"I know what you mean," Tasha said. "I haven't stopped smiling like an idiot since I got here, and I don't even care."

"Where exactly are we?"

Tasha gestured to a formal dining table positioned perfectly in the center of the courtyard. It was covered with a cream-colored silk tablecloth. There were elaborate place settings for at least twenty guests. "At the dinner party, I think."

"Wow," I heard myself say, marveling at the table. "Have you ever seen anything so incredible before?"

"Do you hear that?" Tasha asked. "The music. Someone's playing the piano. It's beautiful."

"*Moonlight Sonata*," I replied. "I hear it."

"There," Tasha said. She pointed toward one of the corners of the courtyard where a beautiful young woman with long auburn hair was playing a white baby grand piano. She was wearing a white dress with silver drops of light that sparkled with every one of her movements. She had on a matching headband keeping her gorgeous hair out of her eyes. She looked up. She caught us staring at her. Tasha and I both blushed. She smiled, urging us to join her with a friendly wave of her hand.

"Who is she?" I asked.

An expression of pure hope filled Tasha's eyes. "Juliet," she answered. My friend moved away from me, practically floating across the glimmering courtyard. She reached the edge of the piano. At once, Juliet moved over on the piano bench, making room for Tasha beside her. Tasha sat down. Even from across the courtyard, I could see awe shining in her eyes.

I turned my attention to movement in the opposite corner. It was Topher. He was sitting on the rounded edge of a white marble fountain, running his hand across the rippling surface of the sparkling water. Behind him a sculpted mermaid was frozen forever, leaping out of the center of the fountain.

Standing nearby was a handsome dark-haired young man who was intensely painting on a canvas propped up on a wooden easel. He stopped what he was doing—like it was an instinct. His paintbrush paused midair, just inches away from the surface of the canvas. The man looked up from his masterpiece-in-progress and was clearly distracted by the sight of Topher sitting there in his burgundy blazer and shiny black shoes. He moved away from the easel and took a step in the direction of the fountain. He seemed captivated by Topher, studying his every movement, like he wanted to memorize them so he could recreate each gesture later. They communicated with their eyes for a moment. Finally, the painter with the curly dark hair moved to Topher and slowly extended his open hand. Topher looked up into the beautiful boy's eyes and smiled. He accepted the painter's hand into his and stood up.

"I'm Pablo," I heard the boy say. I detected some sort of accent in his voice. Italian, maybe.

Topher grinned and replied, "I know who you are."

I turned away and moved to another corner. There I found a different scene. A magic show was in progress. Yet I was the only one watching the performance. My grandfather was wearing the same outfit my Uncle Fred did at the Magic Mansion, complete with the top hat and black floor-length cape lined with crushed red velvet. He looked just as I remembered him with a gray beard and pot belly and an adorable twinkle in his blue eyes.

My grandmother was his reluctant assistant in a scarlet sequined gown, accessorized with a black feathered boa. Her gray hair had a pink tint to it and was piled on top of her head in what looked like an attempt at a beehive hairdo. She was obviously less than thrilled with her role in the show, and this was more apparent when she spoke. "George," she said. "No one wants to watch a magic show."

"And why not?" he asked her.

"Because it's redundant, dear," she explained. "This is Wonderland."

"Ah, yes," he said. "But where do you think the magic comes from?"

My grandmother turned to me. "I give your grandfather a hard time because he expects me to." I smiled at her. "But if you want the truth, I wouldn't want to be anywhere else. Your great-aunt is the mastermind behind all of this. Adrianna hired us as the entertainment for these dinner parties she has. I'm no Connie Francis, but then again, he's no Harry Houdini."

"I miss you, Grandma," I said, feeling a few tears slide

down my cheeks. I stepped forward, wanting to hug her. She held up a hand to stop me.

"Go," she said. "Love is waiting for you, Destiny."

I moved to the last corner of the courtyard. I stood beneath a crooked string of lanterns. One of them had burnt out, and another was flickering to a slow death. From where I stood, I could see all three scenarios playing out at the same time. Juliet was still playing the piano, serenading all of us with the haunting sounds of Beethoven. Tasha couldn't take her eyes away from Juliet. Topher and Pablo were sitting beside the mermaid fountain, holding hands and staring into each other's eyes. My grandmother was chasing an escaped white rabbit through a bed of marigolds. My grandfather was waving his glitter-tipped magic wand up toward the moon as if writing his initials across the sky with the sparkly silver tip.

I stood alone, waiting for the unknown. I was nervous. I was starting to sweat. I desperately needed something to drink.

For the first time since I'd been inside Wonderland, a thin layer of doubt started invading my thoughts.

Maybe he changed his mind. Maybe he saw you arrive and decided you aren't the one for him. Maybe true love doesn't—

"Destiny?" I felt the word on the back of my neck. "You're wearing my favorite color."

I turned around. Dominic and I stood, face-to-face. "Cobalt blue," I said.

He was just an inch taller than me. His dark brown hair was cut short. His eyes were hazel. Looking into them created a warmth inside my body I'd never felt before.

His Mediterranean skin was smooth and sun-kissed. He looked Italian like Pablo—or maybe he was Spanish or Latino.

"Dominic," I heard myself say. "It's nice to finally meet you."

He reached out and brushed his knuckles softly against my cheek. "Are you real?" he whispered. I shuddered a little when he touched me, when we made physical contact. "You're beautiful."

I shifted nervously in my white high heels. I couldn't stop staring at his mouth. His lips looked like they were begging to be kissed. "I'm real," I said, followed by an awkward giggle. I didn't know what to do with my hands. The ridiculous dress had no pockets.

I should've worn a sweater. Or jeans. Why does he keep staring at me?

I was just as guilty. I couldn't stop staring at him. I was enamored with his every movement, with every breath he took.

Dominic reached for my hand. "May I have this dance?" he asked.

I couldn't speak. I nodded in reply. I placed my palm against his. Our fingers meshed together.

A perfect fit.

Dominic led me to the center of the courtyard. I slipped my arms around his neck. He placed his hands on my waist. We started to dance, swaying to the aching piano Juliet played with the longing she now felt for Tasha.

Over Dominic's shoulder, I spotted a beautiful crystal punch bowl filled with a pink-colored liquid, covered with a top layer of orange slices. I thought about stopping our dance long enough to grab a quick glass, but Adrianna's words rang in my head.

You only get one dance with Dominic.

I knew our time together could end at any moment, without warning. I wanted to enjoy every second I was with him.

I felt safe in his arms. His body was athletic and solid, but not overly muscular.

As if he could read my mind, he said, "Being with you is as wonderful as I expected."

"We only get one dance," I said.

He shook his head. "No. That's not fair. I've waited for you…"

Topher and Pablo joined us in the middle of the courtyard. I watched as they started to dance, lost in each other's gaze. Tasha and Juliet soon followed, oblivious to the world around them.

Arm in arm, my grandparents stood nearby watching with approval.

I shifted my attention back to Dominic, to the incredible way his body felt pressed up against me as we moved together as one. I knew the kiss was coming before our mouths met. But when I felt Dominic's lips against mine, it took my breath away.

"Wow," he said, grinning. "You're incredible."

I realized we weren't alone. Someone was standing behind me. Close. I could sense it. I could feel her presence.

My mother.

"Don't turn around," she said. The sound of her soft voice caused my heart to ache. "If you do, it will all go away."

"Mom?" My voice cracked. I began to cry. "Don't leave me."

"Destiny," she said. "You have to make a choice soon."

I felt Dominic's fingertip on my cheek when he brushed away my tears. We looked into each other's eyes, knowing.

I felt my mother's hand on my back offering comfort and reassurance. "I want you to choose love," she said.

I nodded. "I will," I promised.

The music stopped.

The Chinese lanterns flickered and died.

Blackness covered the courtyard, muting the moment.

Before I knew what was happening, I felt my body being lifted into the air with tremendous force as if a giant hand had reached down into the garden and picked me up.

As I ascended above the garden, now shrouded in darkness, I realized Tasha and Topher were in the air beside me. We reached for each other, clutching hands as we continued to rise.

The garden grew faint below us. The twinkle of the stars grew closer above.

Fearing I would never see Dominic again, I closed my eyes.

CHAPTER SIX

My eyes were still shut tight when I heard Tasha's voice cutting through my hazy thoughts. For a moment I wondered if I'd somehow lost consciousness and was just coming to. I was sprawled on my back but had no recollection of how I ended up that way or where I was.

Tasha must've been thinking the same thing. "Where are we?" she said. Her voice was cracked and her throat sounded dry. She wasn't next to me, but pretty close by.

I felt something cold and gritty against the back of my legs, arms, and neck. It was a rough texture pressing against my skin.

I knew we weren't in Wonderland anymore. The dinner party was over before it even really began. No more dances with Dominic. No more magic.

I opened my eyes. I stared up at an empty black swing swaying back and forth above my face. Beyond that I could see a ceiling of stars, blanketed across the August night sky.

I tilted my head. I saw the shiny metal slide. Next to it was the cement tunnel Topher used as his hideaway when Nathan, Boyd, and Skeeter chased him from school.

We're at the playground. But how? Did Adrianna send us here? Are we being punished?

I rolled over in the sand and crawled out from beneath

the swing set. I brushed off the back of my blue party dress. I kicked off my white high heels and scooped them up with my hands.

The playground felt eerie. It was bathed in patches of moonlight and darkness. It didn't seem right to be there after sundown—like something bad could happen to us at any second. I tried to ignore the tickle of fear tumbling through my veins.

"I think we crash-landed," I said. My body ached from head to toe.

Tasha was lying on her side a few feet away. Her face was turned toward the harbor. I could see the shoreline in the distance. The moon was reflected on the surface of the slow, rolling waves. Like the playground, the beach was deserted. Not a soul in sight.

I went to Tasha and knelt beside her. I touched her arm. "Are you okay?" I asked.

"I hurt," she said. "And I think I ate sand."

Tasha turned over and sat up. Her hair was a windblown mess. I reached out and smoothed it down and back into place. The front of her dress had a tear in it. A piece of the peach chiffon material was missing. "Do I look as awful as I feel?" she asked.

"You're as gorgeous as ever," I lied.

Tasha reached for me, grabbing my hand. "Did you see her?" she asked. There was a glimmer of panic in her eyes. "Juliet? Was she real?"

"I don't know," I answered. "Is any of this? I mean, did all of that just really happen?"

Another voice cut across the playground, coming to us from somewhere in the distance. The sharp urgency in the words chilled me. "You can't talk about it."

Tasha hurried to her feet. She stood in front of me as if

it were her instinct to protect me. "Who's there?" she called out.

A pink-haired, tattooed figure in fishnet tights, a plaid skirt, tank top, and black combat boots stepped out from the shadows and into the pit of sand.

"Bettina," I heard myself say.

"Don't look so surprised, love child," she said to me. "I told you…I have a gift."

Tasha rolled her eyes and let out a small laugh. "The only gift you have is not being caught yet for conning people," she said. "Leave us alone, Bettina. We're in the middle of something here."

"You can drop the tough-girl act," Bettina told her. "I've known you since you were in diapers, Tasha Gordon. You're no bad girl. No matter how hard you try."

"And you are?" Tasha threw back at her.

"Don't worry," Bettina said to us. "Your secrets are safe with me."

"We don't have any secrets," I said, still standing behind Tasha.

"Yes, we do," Tasha countered. She folded her arms across her chest and gave Bettina a look. "Talk," she insisted. "Tell us what you know."

Bettina shook her head. "That's just the thing," she said. "You can't tell anybody about what you experienced tonight. You both know better. Adrianna was very clear."

"How do you know what happened?" I asked.

"Yeah," Tasha added. "You weren't there."

Bettina tapped an index finger against her temple. "I saw everything."

"You're bluffing," Tasha said, shaking her head.

Bettina held up a ring of keys in her hand, dangling them. A silver one caught a glint of moonlight. My eyes shifted to

Bettina's black nail polish and back to the keys. "Am I?" she asked.

"What are those?" I asked Tasha.

"The keys to my stepfather's pickup truck."

"That doesn't prove anything, Bettina," I said. "You could've stolen the truck from where Tasha parked it."

"No, Destiny," Tasha said. "She couldn't have. Because the keys were in my pocket when we walked into Wonderland."

"Maybe now it's all becoming clear," Bettina said. "Why am I here. Who sent me. My purpose. I have information for you. For all three of you."

"We don't want any," I said.

"Yes, you do," she answered. "So stop looking at me like you want to shoot me, love child. I'm just—"

"The messenger," Tasha completed.

Bettina locked eyes with her. "Exactly."

I moved closer to Tasha. "Where's Topher?" I asked.

In response, he poked his head out of an open end of the tunnel. "I'm in here," he said.

"Of course you are," Bettina said, sounding slightly annoyed. "You can come out now, scaredy-cat."

"Don't call him that," Tasha warned. "He gets enough grief from your brother."

"Let's leave Boyd out of this," Bettina said.

Topher emerged from his hiding spot and stood next to Tasha. "Good idea," he agreed.

"Wait," I said, "Bettina, you're related to one of those Neanderthals who chase Topher every day?"

She shot me a look. "He's my brother. What do you want me to do about it?"

"Um…counseling. Medication. Anger management classes," I suggested. "Juvenile hall."

"Look, he doesn't listen to anyone. Not even me. He does

his own thing. Topher knows I'm cool with him being gay," she explained.

"You have five seconds to explain what you're doing here," Tasha informed her.

"I was sent here," she replied. "For your own good. There's things you don't know."

"You expect us to believe Adrianna let you into Wonderland?" I asked. "She wouldn't do that."

"She and I made a deal."

"I bet you did," Tasha said. "What's in it for you, Bettina?"

"She said I needed to prove myself to her."

"How?" I said. "By stalking us at the playground?"

"By explaining the rules to the three of you."

"I thought there were none," I challenged.

"You know better than that, love child," she said. "You of all people should know about consequences."

Tasha was frustrated. "You're talking in circles, Bettina. Just tell us what you know."

"Not here," she said. "It's not safe."

"Where then?" Tasha asked.

"The Magic Mansion," she instructed. "Meet me in fifteen minutes. And don't be late."

"Choose another place," Tasha said. "I had to turn my key in when Sir Frederic the Great had to let me go. We don't have a way in."

Bettina looked at me. "Yes, we do."

I stared at her, confused. "Are you crazy? I don't have a key."

Bettina came to me. She reached a hand out toward my throat. I felt her fingers brush against my skin. I looked down. Hanging around my neck on a thin silver chain was a key. Where it came from, I had no idea.

"Liar," Bettina said, grinning. She held up the key with the palm of her hand. "Adrianna took care of everything. You have the key. Tasha knows the alarm code. Topher knows how to work the lights."

"I won't do it," I said. "My uncles trust me. I just moved here. I won't jeopardize—"

Bettina looked into my eyes. I could feel her words on my mouth, her breath. "If you want to see Dominic again, you will."

❖

Tasha's hands were trembling when she slid the key into the ignition of the pickup truck. The three of us were crammed together, shoulder to shoulder, with Topher sitting in the middle. I rolled down the window beside me, desperate for some fresh air.

"I'm still shaking," Tasha told us. "Ever since we left the dinner party. My body feels strange."

"I know what you mean," Topher said. "It's like a nervous energy."

We pulled away from the parking spot where we'd found the truck just moments ago, beneath a palm tree near a closed bicycle rental stand painted banana yellow. The wheels on the truck vibrated as Tasha drove slowly down a cobblestoned street.

"What if she's lying?" I said. "What if Bettina followed us there? She probably has no idea about what really happened to us. She's making it up."

"But what if she's not?" Tasha said. "Think about how we left Wonderland. We didn't even get to say good-bye."

"I want to go back," Topher said. "I want to talk to Adrianna."

I agreed with him. "So do I."

"Don't you think if Adrianna wanted us to be there she'd find a way to make it possible?" Tasha said.

"But why include Bettina?" I asked. "It doesn't make any sense."

"Maybe she's telling the truth," Tasha suggested. "Maybe Adrianna really is testing her."

"Or maybe she's testing *us*," Topher said.

I looked at him, his profile. "What do you mean?"

"I don't think we're supposed to tell anybody," he said. "Not just about Wonderland, but about the stuff that happens there."

"No one would believe us if we did," Tasha said. "This entire island would think we were psycho."

I shrugged. "Maybe we are."

"Don't say that," Topher said. "Tonight was the best night of my life."

"Mine, too," Tasha added.

"I miss him already," I confessed.

"You guys look *so* hot together," Tasha said. I could hear the smile in her voice. I glanced over at her to see if I was right. Sure enough, she was grinning from ear to ear.

"Pablo is perfect," Topher said. "It's like Adrianna snuck inside my mind. She knew exactly the type of person I wanted to meet...to fall in love with."

"But why us?" I said. "And why now? I mean, why not just wait until school starts next week? I'm sure the three of us would've eventually met them somehow."

Tasha shook her head. "I've never seen them before."

"Me either," Topher added. "I don't think they go to our school."

Tasha parked the truck a block away from the Magic Mansion. "Yeah," she said. "Maybe they're from Charleston."

My hand was on the door handle, ready to open it. "What's the plan?" I asked. "Are we really going inside?"

Tasha and Topher looked at me. He nodded and she spoke. "Do we even have a choice?"

❖

A few minutes later, the three of us were sitting on wooden folding chairs in the front row of the tiny, chilly theater. Bettina faced us, perched on the edge of the stage beneath the stark glow of a pale work light Topher had switched on seconds after we arrived. Her hands were braced on the lip of the stage, as if she were a swimmer about to dive into the water. Her shoulders were bent forward. I watched the slow, steady sway of her left foot as she subconsciously tapped against the apron of the stage with the back of her war-torn boot. She looked like the lead singer of some all-girl rock band who'd been forced by her manager to sit in front of her audience to take mind-numbing post-show questions from the crowd.

I glanced around the dimly lit room, at the sea blue walls, the bold red stage curtains sprinkled with gold and silver shiny stars, the grids of lights hanging above. For a moment, I could almost see my grandparents onstage: my grandfather as the star of the show in his cape and top hat being helped by his obligated assistant, my eye-rolling grandmother in a sequined gown, busy patting the back of her cotton candy hairdo and humming a Connie Francis tune.

What was it like back then—this place? When times were better, was every seat filled? Were people amazed by what they saw onstage? It's so beautiful in here. What happens if Uncle Fred and Clark lose it? No. The Magic Mansion can't close. I won't let it happen.

"What I'm about to tell you can never leave this room,"

Bettina said with an authoritative tone I hadn't heard her use before. "Do you understand me?"

The three of us nodded obediently in unison.

"I followed you to Wonderland," she said.

I gave Tasha a look and mouthed the words "I told you so."

Topher pinched my arm to settle me down. I turned back to Bettina the Big Liar and waited for her to continue.

"I tried to get in," she said. "Like I've tried before. I wasn't expecting to because it's usually a no-go…but then it happened…the door opened. I went inside."

"We didn't see you there," Tasha said, a thick layer of doubt coating her words.

"The three of you were already gone."

"Gone?" Topher echoed.

"At the dinner party. At least that's where she said you were."

"Go on," I prompted. My stomach growled to remind me none of us had actually eaten any *food* at the dinner party. I was starving, but it wasn't exactly the right moment to suggest we order a pizza.

"Adrianna said she had something very important for me to do," Bettina continued. "If I helped her and did what I was told, she would consider inviting me back to Wonderland."

"So basically you're using us?" Tasha said. "To return to Wonderland?"

"Put it however you want, Tasha. Do you wanna know what she told me or not?"

Tasha folded her arms across her chest. "Tell us."

"You're each going back to Wonderland," she said.

"When?" I asked.

"She didn't say exactly."

"Well, what *did* she say?" Tasha asked.

"A few days. She said it would be a few days. But you have to be prepared. She made that very clear."

"What happens when we go back?" I asked.

"Will the others be there?" Topher said. "Do we get to see them again before school starts?"

"She said that each of you will have to make a choice," Bettina said.

I sat up in the uncomfortable chair. "She told me the same thing," I offered. "So did…my mother."

"When you get there you'll be asked to decide."

"Decide about what?" Tasha asked.

"Yeah, what are we choosing between?" Topher wanted to know.

My great-aunt's words floated into my mind. In that moment, I knew. I felt a chill go down my spine. "Between life and death," I said.

Bettina looked in my direction with her heavily outlined eyes. "Destiny is right," she said. "Adrianna said so."

"You mean we have to decide if we want to live or die?" Topher asked. "No, she wouldn't do that to us."

"It's not about us," I said. "It's about people we love. People who are already gone."

"You mean, like your mom?" Tasha said.

I nodded, trying to ignore the urge to cry. "Yeah. I think so."

Bettina's foot finally stopped moving. "It's more complicated than that," she said.

Tasha's body tensed. "Explain."

"She wouldn't tell me everything, but she gave me a sense of how Wonderland works."

"We're listening," I said.

"When people arrive at Wonderland they're either alive or dead," Bettina said. "In our case, we're all alive. But some of the others that are there…they've been given a second chance."

"To do what?" Topher asked.

Bettina looked into our eyes. It felt like she was trying to read our minds. I wondered if this was a tactic she used on her unsuspecting customers who came to her convinced she could see into their future. It was effective. I was starting to believe her. "To change their fate," she said. "Their outcome."

I stood up partly because the wooden folding chair was hurting my back but mostly because the realization of what Bettina was saying—and what Wonderland was really about—hit me hard. "What you're talking about is crazy," I said.

She raised a pierced eyebrow. "Is it?"

"Magic is one thing," I told her. "But bringing someone back from the dead?"

Tasha and Topher looked up at me. I glanced down at their wide-eyed expressions. "Destiny, what are you saying?" Topher asked.

"We were picked for a specific purpose. A reason," I explained. "Adrianna saw something in the three of us. That's why she brought us to Wonderland. She knew we would believe in it. She said we had to be certain. We had to feel it in our hearts."

"I felt it," Tasha said. "In the courtyard with Juliet. I've never felt that way before about anything."

"Same here," Topher said. "When I was with Pablo… nothing else mattered."

"You don't have to explain it to me," I said. "I know exactly what you guys are talking about. Dominic made me feel…"

"Like you were falling in love?" Bettina asked.

I nodded in reply.

"Maybe the six of you have more in common than you

think," Bettina suggested. "Maybe you each lost somebody who was really important to you."

"Like who?" Tasha asked. "The only person I've ever known who died was my father."

"Maybe Adrianna is going to give you a chance to reconnect with him," I said.

"Why would she?" Tasha said. "I don't mean any disrespect, but his death wasn't exactly a big loss."

"You weren't close to him?" I asked.

"He wasn't close to anybody," she said. "Except Jack Daniel's. He drank himself to death. Got so messed up one night he drove himself into a telephone pole. He died on impact."

"So you wouldn't bring him back?" Topher asked.

Bettina hopped down from the edge of the stage. "I know who I'd bring back," she said. "My grandmother. What about you, Topher?"

"Maybe my dad," he said. "Although I'm not really sure if he's dead or not. No one knows."

Tasha's voice rose when she spoke. Her words were sharp. "Do you guys hear what you're saying? It's one thing to stumble upon some magical house, but bringing someone back from their grave? That's too psycho—even for me."

A voice tumbled across the theater, reaching us. When we heard his words, we knew weren't alone anymore. Our secret meeting in the Magic Mansion had been discovered. "It's not psycho," Clark said. He was standing in the double doorway leading to the lobby and the makeshift gift shop. He was wearing faded jeans, a red button-up cardigan sweater over a white tee, and a pair of old blue Converse. His hair was messy. Maybe he'd woken from a deep sleep and hurried to get here. To find us. To stop us. "I know what it sounds like, but it's true."

I locked eyes with my uncle's beautiful lover and asked, "How do you know, Clark?"

He held my stare, licked his lips, and then said to us, "Because I died two months ago."

CHAPTER SEVEN

I sent Bettina away because she can't be trusted," Clark told the three of us moments later. We were sitting in a circle on the black floor in the center of the empty stage. My vintage party dress surrounded me like a giant blue bubble. My bare feet were tucked beneath me. My white high heels—now scuffed beyond repair—were sitting in the audience in the wooden folding chair I'd occupied just seconds ago.

My friends look exhausted. Tasha sat like a wilted peach blossom in her wrinkled and torn chiffon dress. Topher's blue gray eyes were sleepy and smudged with rings of smeared guyliner. Clark seemed nervous and anxious. I had no idea what time it was, but I was starving and overwhelmed by all I'd experienced since arriving only yesterday. I missed Chicago. I missed Samantha. I even missed my ridiculous little brother. I just wanted my life to feel normal again.

After Clark dropped the major bombshell on us, we stood like open-mouthed zombies just staring at him. We were dazed, not just by the words he'd said, but by all we'd encountered in the course of one night. I didn't know how much more my friends and I could take. It felt like we were riding high on the crest of an emotional tidal wave.

With Clark's arrival—and his crazy confession—I knew the night was far from being over. I wondered how much more bizarre my new world could become. How far would the limits of reality be stretched? Why was my belief in magic being constantly tested in this strange little seaside town?

I'd been in Avalon Cove for just a little over twenty-four hours. Already I'd met my great-aunt who had been dead for over a decade. And her sweet card-playing deceased husband, Alfred, and their smiling orange cat, Montgomery. I danced with a beautiful boy in a fairyland garden at a foodless dinner party where the ghosts of my grandparents were the entertainment. Now my uncle's gay partner had just told me and my two new BFFs he died two months ago, but here he was alive and breathing and sitting with us on the dusty, glittery stage at the Magic Mansion.

And how could I even begin to explain Wonderland? The entire place had been transformed from one visit to the next. What was once a creepy, dilapidated haunted house had become a grand estate bursting with inviting lights. Inside, there was no sense of time or reality.

There was just my gorgeous, glamorous great-aunt and her wild tales of life after death.

Maybe Wonderland exists somewhere between the two. How else could my mother be there? We buried her two weeks ago. I saw her in the casket. I touched her face. I was at the funeral. There's no way she could be alive. She's a ghost. Or whatever it is she's become.

"I have it on a good authority Bettina didn't pass the challenge that was given to her," Clark said. We looked like overgrown kids ready for a late-night version of Duck, Duck, Goose. To my left, I spied a half-eaten carrot lying just off stage. I wondered if Carrots might have gotten out of her cage and was roaming the place. Maybe she'd had enough of a life in show business and wanted to break free.

Tasha's voice brought me back to the conversation

happening around me. "Why not? What did Bettina do wrong?" she asked.

"She lied," he explained.

Surprise, surprise. I knew Bettina the Big Liar wasn't telling the truth.

"To us?" Topher said.

"Yes," said Clark. "But more importantly, she lied to Adrianna."

"Why would she do that?" Topher asked.

"Because she's a big fake," I said. "I told you guys we shouldn't believe her."

"She did it because she's desperate," Clark said. "She's not interested in connecting with her dead grandmother. She's trying to bring back an ex-boyfriend."

"That figures," I said, my anger with Bettina growing by the second.

"The only problem is…he's not dead," Clark explained. "I know it sounds crazy, but he allowed her to believe he was dead to avoid breaking things off with her. From what I hear, she was a bit…possessive…where he was concerned. Some even say she was obsessed. She has his name tattooed on the back of her neck."

"He really did that?" Tasha asked. "But why? Just break up with her and move on."

"Because Bettina isn't a psychic," I said. "She's a *psycho*."

"Let's go easy on Bettina," Clark said. "She's had a tough time in this town."

"All of us have," Tasha reminded him. "We're not exactly part of the popular crowd. Except for Destiny."

"Me?" I said, flashing Tasha a look. "Yeah, right. No one here even knows me. Except for you guys."

"Oh, please," Tasha said. "By the first day of school, you

won't even know who we are. Everyone's going to fall in love with you. Just like Dominic has. You're blond and perfect."

No, I'm not. I'm a complete dork.

"Hey, not all of us are lucky enough to look like Rihanna," I said.

"I *don't* look like her," Tasha protested.

"Yes, you do," Topher and I said at the same time.

"Whatever," Tasha said with an annoyed shrug. "I've lived here all my life. So has Topher. We know how it is. No one likes us. Because we're different."

"It's cool," Topher said. "I'd rather be an outcast. I'd rather just be myself."

"I'm not trying to sound judgmental," I replied. "And you're right, Clark. I don't know Bettina well enough to understand why she'd lie. I just don't trust her. When she showed up at the playground tonight, I knew something had to be in it for her."

"Adrianna gave her an opportunity and she blew it," Clark explained. "Big-time."

"What about us?" I asked. "Are we being punished? Or are we in the clear?"

"No," he said. "Not yet."

"Did we do something wrong?" Topher asked.

Clark glanced at each of us with his deer brown eyes before answering. "The three of you…you can never talk about Wonderland. To no one. Not even to each other," he informed us. "The only reason why I'm here with you right now and why I'm allowed to share with you what I went through is because Adrianna asked me to. She gave me permission to do so, because she cares about you very much."

"And because Bettina almost ruined everything for us?" Tasha added. "She's always been like that. It's all about *her*."

"Adrianna asked me to intervene on her behalf. By

tomorrow morning, Bettina won't remember a thing about tonight. She'll wake up without a clue."

"How's that possible?" I asked. "You're saying her memory will be erased?"

"After what I've witnessed at Wonderland, I can truly say *anything* is possible," he said. "Especially in Adrianna's hands. I'm living proof of that. If it weren't for her, I wouldn't be here."

"Where would you be?" Topher pressed.

"At the bottom of the Atlantic Ocean," he said. "I was in a boating accident two months ago. It happened the first week of summer. I fell overboard. I'm not much of a swimmer. And even though Fred told me to put on a life vest before we left the harbor, I didn't listen."

"So, what happened?" Topher prompted.

Clark took a breath before he spoke. "I died," he said. "I drowned."

"You keep saying that, Clark." Tasha said, as if she'd read my mind. "Um…explain."

"I will," he said. "I promise. But right now we don't have much time."

Clark was right. He'd sent Bettina out to buy us dinner. She'd be back any second with a couple of large pizzas. When Clark insisted she go and get our food, she threw a huge temper tantrum. She refused at first, but he eventually wore her down. He even threatened to tell Adrianna she was unwilling to cooperate. Finally, she relented.

"Normally, I would think you were insane because people just don't come back from the grave after a boating accident," Tasha said, "but I know better than to doubt it. Especially in Avalon Cove."

"What does Adrianna have to do with this?" I asked.

"How else? She brought me to Wonderland," he said. "I don't remember being there, or even meeting her. But I went back to Wonderland to thank her. She said she chose me. She said your uncle showed up right after the accident. Adrianna gave him a choice."

"And he chose you?" Topher asked, smiling again.

Clark's eyes filled with tenderness. "Yes," he said, with a small nod. "He chose me."

"Wow," I said, "I didn't even know you guys owned a boat."

You're such an idiot, Destiny. Who says something so lame at a time like this? Clark's looking at you like you're totally insensitive.

In that moment, I remembered Clark standing beside me at the cemetery, reaching for my hand. He gave it a gentle squeeze as they lowered my mother's casket into the ground. As if he were trying to let me know that everything was going to be okay.

"We don't. Not anymore," he said. "After I drowned, your uncle got rid of the thing. Sold it to a family from Hilton Head."

"But we would've heard about the accident," Tasha said. "This is a small island. When something like that happens, everybody knows about it."

"That's just it," he said. "Because Fred chose me, the accident actually never happened."

"Now you're really confusing me," Tasha said.

"He went back. Fred changed things."

Tasha turned to me. "Is this making any sense to you?"

I shook my head. "No. I feel like I'm in *The Twilight Zone*. I have since I got here yesterday. This entire island is nuts, if you ask me."

"I know it all sounds crazy," Clark agreed, "but Bettina will be back soon, and I need to tell you things before she does."

"We're listening," I said.

"In three days you're each going back to Wonderland. When you get there, you're going to be given a choice."

"To bring someone back?" Topher asked. "Like Destiny's mom?"

Clark looked at me. "It won't be that simple," he said. "It's not what you think."

"Then what is it?" I asked.

"It will be different for each of you," he continued. "None of you will have the same journey. But the decision will be just as hard. Adrianna's going to give you a chance...to make things right."

"You mean to actually go back...in time...and save someone's life?" I asked. "You're talking about changing fate."

Clark nodded. "That's exactly what will happen."

"What if we're not supposed to? I mean, how do we know if we're making the right choice?" I said.

"You don't," he answered. "There's no guarantee. You have to go with your heart. Listen to what it tells you to do. That's very important."

"How long will we have to decide?" I asked.

"Not long. Maybe a matter of seconds. So be prepared."

"How can we do that?" Tasha asked.

"Spend the next couple of days doing your research," he told us.

"Research?" Topher repeated. "Is this like a homework assignment? Are we writing a term paper?"

"Don't be dumb, Topher," Tasha said.

"I suggest each of you find out everything you can about the three people you met tonight. Find out who they are, where they come from. This information might be crucial to you later."

"I wouldn't even know where to begin," I said. "I only know his name."

"We can help you, Destiny," Topher offered. "Tasha and me can be very resourceful."

"What Topher's trying to say is we've have a little bit of experience in…stalking," Tasha confessed.

"The three of us can work together," I said. "We can help each other."

"But no matter what, after tonight…you can't breathe a word of this to anyone." Clark's eyes rested on me. "Not even Uncle Fred. There will be consequences if you tell someone about Wonderland."

"What kind of consequences?" Topher asked. He looked scared.

"Tough ones," Clark said. "Everything can be taken away in a second. The choice you make…if you tell anyone, it can be undone. Wonderland must appear to everyone else as you each saw it the first time you arrived. It's nothing more than an abandoned old house that the entire island swears is haunted. It will never be sold or demolished or entered into by anyone except those who have been invited."

"How is that even possible? I mean, a lot of people love old houses. And the architecture is amazing. Someone with a lot of money could come along and make an offer—"

"Wonderland will always be exactly what it is," he said. "It can never change. It won't. Because your uncle owns the property."

"My grandfather…he left everything to Uncle Fred?" I asked.

"The Magic Mansion," he said. "And Wonderland. Both places must *always* stay in your family."

I realized why I was now living in Avalon Cove. Everything made perfect sense. I knew the answer to my question, but I had to ask anyway. I had to hear Clark say the words. "And once my uncle's gone," I said, "what happens then?"

Clark locked eyes with mine. "They become yours, Destiny."

CHAPTER EIGHT

*I*t's your legacy.

Those were the words Clark said to me when he drove us home from the Magic Mansion. After devouring half a pizza, shooting Bettina death rays from my very tired eyes, and trying to shake off my plaguing homesickness for Chicago, the last thing I wanted to think about was a legacy. It wasn't my fault my mother's family possessed some strange supernatural powers.

What if I don't want the legacy? What if I refuse to be next in line? What if I sold the Magic Mansion and Wonderland just to prove a point? I could put an end to this craziness. I didn't ask to be born into this bizarre family.

I was certain Clark could sense my mood.

He glanced over at me before shifting his eyes back to the road. A light rain had started to fall, misting the windshield. He clicked on the wipers. They moved slow and steady, back and forth, giving off a faint squeak. "This is a lot for you to deal with," he said.

My shoulders ached. "You think?" I said. "I haven't even unpacked yet. Couldn't we have waited until school started before springing on me that my relatives are freaks of nature?"

"I'm sorry this is all happening so fast, Destiny."

I nodded. I looked out the passenger window. "Me too."

"Adrianna saw something in you," he said. "So did your grandfather."

"How?" I asked. "They don't even know me. None of you really do."

"It might not seem like it," Clark said, "but we're family."

The rain started to hit harder. "Maybe," I said. "Or maybe this was all planned. I mean, did my mother have to die just so I could come to Avalon Cove? Did I have to actually be here in order to learn about my legacy, as you call it?"

"No. What happened to your mother was a tragedy," he said. "I know you miss her."

"You have no idea."

"Maybe you'll see her again," he said. "Or maybe you already have."

"Is that what I'm supposed to do? Is that the choice I need to make? To bring my mother back?"

"I can't tell you that."

"Well, what *can* you tell me, Clark?"

"What would you like to know?"

"I don't know…something that doesn't sound completely insane. Anything that doesn't deal with ghosts or bringing people back from the dead."

"You're angry."

"You're right," I said. "Why does it have to be me? Why can't I just be a normal girl with guy problems?"

"Because that's not who you are," he said. "You're special."

"Well, I don't wanna be. Right now, I just wanna go home."

Clark braked softly at a stop sign and said, "We're almost there."

"I'm talking about Chicago," I said. "No offense, but coming here wasn't my decision. I didn't exactly have a say in where I was going."

"We're happy you're here," he reminded me. "I promise you."

I suddenly felt like a complete jerk. Clark had been nothing but nice to me and here I was acting like a spoiled brat. "I'm sorry," I said. "It's not you. You've been so sweet to me. It's just…all of this is really new. The island. Living with you and Uncle Fred. Being at Wonderland…with Dominic."

Clark raised an eyebrow. "Dominic?" he repeated. "Do tell."

"There's not much to say."

"I don't believe you," he said. "Your eyes lit up when you said his name."

I hoped Clark couldn't tell I was blushing. I was grateful it was dark inside the car, except for the faint glow from the dashboard. "We spent all of five minutes together," I said, then added, "but it was enough."

"You like him?"

We pulled up in front of the house. I stared through the car window at the porch swing, the ceramic pigs, and the well-manicured lawn. A light downstairs was on. Uncle Fred was probably waiting up for us.

I reached for the door handle and said, "It's worse. I think I'm in love."

❖

As I'd predicted, Uncle Fred was wide awake and waiting for us when we walked in. He was pacing in the living room in a red robe and striped pajamas. He looked exhausted. I felt bad for keeping him up.

The clock on the wall said it was almost midnight. I'd made it home just before my curfew, thanks to Clark.

"I thought you were dead," my uncle said to me. He turned to Clark with a reprimanding stare. "Both of you. I thought both of you were dead. Clark, do you realize you've been gone for almost two hours?"

He thought we died? Is anybody really dead on this island? Do they even have funerals here?

"We're both fine," Clark said. "Stop worrying."

"I can't help it," Uncle Fred admitted. "You two are all I have." He looked at me. "Now I can see you're alive with my own eyes, how was the dinner party?"

I avoided his questioning gaze. "Overwhelming," I said.

"I bet."

"You just need a good night's rest," Clark suggested.

"It's good to be home," I said, heading to the stairs. "I've been in this dress and these heels for hours. I'm disgusting. I need a bath."

"Let's put you to bed, Sir Frederic the Great," Clark said. I could hear the smile in his voice. My uncle protested at first, insisting he wasn't tired. But Clark convinced him otherwise.

Upstairs, I flipped on the lights, stripped off my clothes, and climbed into a cool bath. Immediately, my body felt revived. I shut off the water, closed my eyes, and focused on the *drip drip drip* sound caused by an occasional heavy drop falling from the faucet and hitting the still surface.

I tried to imagine what life was like for my mother while she was growing up in Avalon Cove. Did she love the island? When did she make up her mind to leave? What motivated her to pursue her dream of becoming a dancer? And what made her change her mind and give up? Meeting my father? Having me? My mother could've had a professional career. She could've toured the world, joined a dance company, pirouetted her way onto a Broadway stage. But none of that happened for her. Instead, she died a divorced woman trying to make ends meet by teaching uncoordinated housewives how to cha-cha in a stuffy dance studio in Chicago.

How come you never told me about Wonderland, Mom? What other secrets did you keep from me?

If my mother hadn't died—if she was still here with us—what would her life be like? If I could go back in time and somehow stop the cancer from spreading, would it make a difference? Would I still hear her cry at night sometimes in her bedroom when she thought I was already asleep?

The walls in that apartment were so thin, Mom. I could hear your pain coming through. I know my father broke your heart. I know you were scared taking care of me and Ian. I could've helped you. I should have...

I'd felt her presence in the garden at Wonderland, her hand on my back. Her spirit. Her words echoed in my brain. *I want you to choose love.*

I'd made a promise to her. *I will.*

But what did that mean? What exactly was I supposed to do? Bring her back like my Uncle Fred had with Clark? Like Adrianna had with her beloved Alfred?

Dominic's beautiful face suddenly flashed in my mind. I could see his kissable lips, his soulful eyes, and his dark brown hair I wanted to run my fingers through. I could almost hear his deep but gentle voice, saying my name. I could feel his body pressed up against mine. His touch. Already, I wanted to see him again—in the flesh and not just in my imagination.

Where are you, Dominic? School doesn't start for another week. I'm not sure if I can wait that long. Come find me. Let's spend every second together we can before September begins and summer ends.

I pinched my nostrils closed and slid under the water. I

thought about tempting my own fate by letting go, breathing in, and surrendering to the unknown. Would I be saved? Would I arrive moments later on the second floor of Wonderland? Would I spend eternity in the kaleidoscope garden watching endless magic shows performed by my grandparents?

I decided not to take my chances. I came up for air.

❖

A half hour later, Clark joined me on the front porch and handed me a mug of peppermint tea. We sat together in the porch swing. The rhythm of the summer rain was steady. The humidity in the air was slowly dissipating. The night was cooling off.

"Did you finally convince Uncle Fred to go to bed?" I asked.

"Sir Frederic is all tucked in and sleeping like a temperamental baby," he said. "He put up a good fight, but I won the battle. I threatened to cut him off from *Wheel of Fortune* if he didn't do what he was told."

"You two are cute together," I said. "You must love each other a lot."

"We do," Clark said with a nod. "But it's not always easy."

"Because you gave up culinary school to be here?" I asked.

"No. I don't regret that. I'm worried about the future of the Magic Mansion. I don't know how much longer we can keep the place going. People just don't want to see magic shows anymore, I guess. They think we're old-fashioned. They've given up on magic."

"What should we do?" I asked.

He shrugged. "Just hope. Not much more we can do."

"What you said earlier…about the Magic Mansion and Wonderland being my legacy," I said. "I can't figure it out and I keep trying to. I mean, why *me*? Why not give it all to my brother? Ian's a boy. Yes, he's kind of a jerk sometimes and all he really cares about is soccer and video games, but I don't know the first thing about running a business."

"It's not about that," he said. "Clearly, they saw something in you."

"How?"

"Your grandfather and his sister are no ordinary people."

"Do they have some sort of super powers?"

"I don't know," he said.

"Obviously they do. You wouldn't be sitting here without them, Clark."

"Before I ended up at Wonderland I never would've believed anything like this was possible."

"I can't make any sense of it," I said. "I've tried to, but nothing I've ever learned in science class can explain what's happening."

"Did you know they were twins?" he asked. I shook my head. "Your grandfather and your great-aunt were very close. I imagine they still are. When they were alive…they were quite the characters. A lot of people in Avalon Cove thought they were strange. Gave 'em a real hard time. He was a magician. She looked like a movie star. No one could figure out why the two of them stayed. According to what your uncle told me, they used to say the same thing about your mother. That she didn't belong here. She was too special for a place like this. Everyone wanted her to go and see the world."

I reached behind the swaying porch swing and slid my hand through a sheet of falling rain. I was surprised by how warm the water was. "Maybe that's why she left," I said, watching rain fill my palm before sliding down my arm. "And that's why she made sure I ended up here. Like maybe she wasn't finished with this place. Maybe there's something I'm supposed to do while I'm here—something besides fall in love with Dominic."

"What's there to finish?" he asked. "She left here a long time ago and never looked back. She met your father. She had a family. She spent her life doing something she really loved."

"Uncle Fred is the same—he has you. This house. The Magic Mansion. His life is fulfilled."

A strange expression crept over Clark's face. "He almost lost it all," he said.

"The boating accident?"

"I guess it wasn't my time to go," Clark said. "That's what Adrianna told him. He went to Wonderland. He knew she would be there. He asked for her help. One minute he and I were on the boat. The next thing I remember I was waking up on the beach."

"What did you do?" I asked.

"I stood up," he said, "and I walked here. I found your uncle sitting in the recliner in the living room watching *Wheel of Fortune*, bawling his eyes out. He couldn't believe I was back, that I'd come home. It was like the accident never even happened. We just went on with our lives as usual."

"You don't remember any of it?" I asked.

"No. Not a thing."

"Then how do you know it actually happened?"

"Simple," he said. "Because I believe."

❖

The next morning there was a knock at my bedroom door. I opened my eyes and was nearly blinded by the different shades of pink surrounding me.

I desperately need to redecorate this room. I feel like I'm trapped inside Barbie's Dream House. What time is it?

My uncle was standing in the open doorway. "Morning," he greeted with his hand on the door knob. He was already showered and dressed for the day in khakis and a black polo shirt.

I squinted. "You look different," I said. "Your hair. You're not wearing it. And you trimmed your mustache."

"I decided to go natural today," he said. "Clark says bald is sexy."

"I like it," I said, trying to form a smile. Uncle Fred looked years younger. He no longer resembled a man you'd see on a cheesy TV commercial trying to sell used cars.

"Thank you," he replied. "Clark says you hate your bedroom."

"I don't hate it," I said. "It's just not me. It's very… pink."

"It's my fault," he said.

"I know."

"A fresh coat of paint and a new bedspread and the room will look like new."

"It's fine…really. I can learn to love the color. And the stuffed animals. Maybe this will all grow on me."

"I'm going to train you today."

"Train me?" I said. I sat up in bed.

"At the Magic Mansion," he explained. "Since you'll be inheriting it one day."

Don't remind me.

"Clark already showed me how to run the gift shop," I explained. "I think I even mastered that archaic beast of a cash register."

"You've been promoted," he decided.

I gave him a look. "I have?"

"Get up. Get dressed. Clark made pancakes. To celebrate."

We had pancakes yesterday. What were we celebrating then? Maybe these are magic pancakes and they eat them every day. Maybe I will have a few and forget about how strange my life has become. Wait. What are we celebrating? I should ask.

"What exactly are we celebrating?"

Uncle Fred's smile was contagious. "You're going to be my new assistant."

I threw back the pink bedspread and tossed a sparkly *Princess* pillow aside. "Uncle Fred, when you say *assistant*, you mean answering the phone and selling tickets and cleaning out bunny cages, right?"

He shook his head. "No, no, no," he said. "I had a vision last night."

"Uh-oh."

"And it makes perfect sense. Even Clark agrees."

"It does?" I said. "He did?"

My kooky uncle smacked his hands together and announced, "I'm putting you in the show!"

My mouth went dry. "What?" I croaked.

He lifted his eyes as if he were staring up at a marquee. "Sir Frederic the Great and his lovely assistant...Destiny!"

You can't be serious. Me? Onstage. Is my brother behind this? Did Ian give his allowance to someone to see me publicly humiliated? I need to call Aunt Barbara and tell her to severely punish him.

"Uncle Fred, that's very nice of you...but...I'm not very... lovely," I offered. "Maybe another girl would be better for the job. What about Tasha? She'd be perfect."

"Nonsense," he said. "You're my niece. Magic is in your blood."

❖

There were more secrets to the magic tricks than I could possibly remember. I followed my uncle diligently, scribbling down notes in a spiral bound notebook while he rattled off random thoughts and words of advice. We moved through the Magic Mansion at a fast pace. It was tough to keep up.

That morning, I was immersed into a world of cranky rabbits, colorful scarves, trapdoors, hidden compartments, and optical illusions. Within a matter of minutes, I realized the magic at the Magic Mansion wasn't so real after all.

This was definitely no Wonderland.

Sometimes, your job is to distract the audience, Destiny.

Got it.

You have remember to smile. Never forget.

Yes, sir.

The show must always go on.

No matter what?

No matter what.

Uncle Fred stopped in his tracks. I wondered if the training was over. Surely there had to be more to it than was covered in a thirty-minute tutorial.

I will never remember all of this. I will be the worst assistant in the history of magic. People will ask for their money back. What's the refund policy in this place?

Uncle Fred glanced over at me, his eyes moving up and down. He was inspecting me. "Go see Bettina," he decided.

"For what?" I asked.

Bettina the Big Liar is the last person I want to see this morning.

"You need an outfit and I don't have one," he explained.

"Nothing too grown-up since you're only fifteen, but you need something flashy, glamorous. You need to look like a star."

I thought about my grandmother in the Wonderland garden. I thought about my great-aunt and her goddess-like presence. I thought about my mother dancing in her jazz shoes and favorite rose-colored pleated skirt and peasant blouse. I could never be like them. Something indescribable radiated from within them—something I knew I didn't have.

"Uncle Fred, I don't want you to be disappointed in me," I said.

He opened his wallet, fished out a few bills, and handed them to me. "Why would you say that?"

"I'm not sure if I'm up for this job," I explained. "I don't want to let you down."

He looked at me with tenderness in his eyes. "You won't, Destiny," he said. "You could never disappoint me."

"How can you be so sure? I mean, my last job was selling cotton candy and corn dogs at Navy Pier. This is different. This is important work. What if I ruin one of your magic tricks?"

"You're right," he said, nodding. "This is very important work. It's unlike anything else in the world. Just wait and see. You're going to fall in love with magic like the rest of us."

"I just…don't want to mess this up," I said. "I know you're struggling to keep this place open. I don't want to be the reason why you have to close it."

My uncle slid his arm around my shoulders and gave me a reassuring squeeze. "The women in my family have been a part of the magic shows for generations," he said.

"What if I'm the exception?" I asked.

He smiled at me. "And what if you're not?"

❖

It was a five-block walk to Bettina's. I got lost. I stopped once I realized I'd missed a turn, went back, and eventually found my way there. I still couldn't figure out the geography of Avalon Cove, at least not the village-like business section. Every cobblestoned street looked the same to me.

It wasn't even noon and already it was unbelievably hot and humid. My body was covered with a thin layer of perspiration by the time I entered the overstocked boutique. Outside, the air was sticky and damp. Inside, I was greeted by a cool blast from the air conditioner. I sighed in relief.

The store was empty, not a customer in sight. A haze of strawberry incense smoke caused my eyes to burn.

A sleepy-looking Bettina stepped out from behind the glass counter. She was wearing a leather studded collar, a ratty black T-shirt, a red vinyl miniskirt, fishnet tights, and her scuffed combat boots. I wondered how much effort it took to look like her. I hoped Clark was right—that she'd woken up that morning with no memory of what had occurred last night.

His theory was confirmed when she asked, "How was your dinner party, love child?"

I stared into her icy blue eyes, trying to detect any hint of deceit. "You're the one with the gift," I said, with caution. "You tell me how you think it went." I folded my arms across my chest and waited for her response.

She looked annoyed with me. I was already irritating her and I'd only arrived. "I have better things to do than sit around all day and night thinking about your boring love life," she informed me.

Clark was right. She has no clue about what happened. Not even about the pizzas we scarfed down at her expense. I can only imagine the look on her face when she finds the receipts in her purse. Maybe she'll convince herself she's crazy. Probably wouldn't be hard.

"Fair enough," I said with a small shrug. "I'm perfectly fine with being boring. You should try it some time. You'll realize you don't need pink hair and tattoos and piercings to make a statement. It's not about what you look like."

"Easy for you to say," she said, her voice frosty.

"You say you have a gift," I said, "but clearly there's a lot you don't know, Bettina."

She stepped toward me with a smug half-grin. "I do know one thing for sure," she said. "You're going back to Wonderland in three days."

She's testing you. Don't let it show. Act like you don't care. It's no big deal.

"Oh yeah? Who told you that?"

She grinned. "The universe did."

I think I rolled my eyes. "Yeah, right."

"Believe whatever you want about me. I don't really care," she said.

"It's not my business if you lie to people," I replied. "That's your karma, not mine."

"Let me explain something to you. I don't take money unless my vision is clear. I'm not a palm reader. I don't tell people what they want to hear. I speak the truth."

I was in no mood to argue with Bettina. I needed to pick out a dress and return to the Magic Mansion so I could resume my training. And later, I needed to find Tasha and Topher to come up with a plan, to decide how each of us was going to take Clark's advice and research Dominic, Pablo, and Juliet. Secretly, I was hoping our little investigation would actually lead us to them. I really, really wanted to see Dominic again. The sooner, the better.

I knew I had to try a different approach with Bettina. I

softencd my tone and said, "Actually, I think you like being different."

She raised an eyebrow—the one that wasn't pierced. "Maybe I do."

"That's probably why Tasha and Topher come around."

"You mean besides the discount I give 'em?" she said.

"No," I said, "because they don't fit in either."

"I'm not an idiot. I know most people don't like me."

"But you prefer it that way," I realized. "It keeps people away from you."

"What are you, my shrink?" she said. "You're just a kid. You don't know anything about life yet."

"Don't underestimate me, Bettina," I said.

"Am I supposed to be scared of you because you come from Chicago?"

"Am I supposed to be intimidated by you just because of how you dress? You act *so* tough, Bettina. But that's all it is… an *act*."

She put a hand on her hip. I was exasperating her. I could tell. "You know, your mother was much…*nicer* to me than you are. She didn't have such an awful attitude."

"We're different people," I said. "Maybe she was easier to fool."

"I have nothing to prove to you, Destiny Moore," she said. "Or to anyone in this town, for that matter."

"I didn't come here to fight," I said. "I need a dress."

She returned to her position behind the counter. "I know," she said. "For your new job. To be a magician's assistant. I wonder how long it'll be before you screw that one up."

I felt a tickle of nerves inside my body.

She knows more than she's letting on.

"What did you just say?" I asked.

"You heard me."

Maybe I'm wrong about Bettina. Maybe we all are. What if she really does have a gift?

She broke the silence between us. "Don't just stand there looking at me like that," she said. "I've been expecting you. I picked out three dresses in your size. They're hanging up in the dressing room. I suggest going with the black one. I like the spaghetti straps on it. But with your perfect skin tone, you're the kind of girl who can get away with wearing anything."

Wait. Did she just compliment me?

I stood there feeling awkward and strange. "I don't know what to say."

"You can start with thank you," she said. "Then later you can work up to *I'm sorry I doubted you, Bettina.*"

"I don't know if that will ever happen," I said.

"Yeah," she replied, "I won't hold my breath."

"What you said earlier about my mom...I think you're right. She *was* a nicer person than I am."

I turned and made my way to the dressing room, pulling the slatted door shut behind me. Sure enough, there were three dresses inside hanging from a metal hook screwed in to the back of the door. I reached for the black one on instinct. I had to try it on just to be sure. Yet I already knew it would be a perfect fit.

Because Bettina said so.

Changing clothes in the tiny room was difficult. The space was no bigger than a broom closet. I was surrounded by own reflection, catching glimpses of myself each direction I moved.

Once I had the dress on, I stared at myself in the mirror.

Damn. She's right. Don't bother trying on the other two. This one's it.

"I'll take the black," I said loudly, hoping Bettina would hear me wherever she was in the store. She didn't respond.

I slid the beautiful knee-length dress back onto the plastic hanger. "Bettina," I said, hoping my words would filter through the tiny spaces between the wooden slats in the dressing room door. "I give up. You were right. The dress is perfect."

I listened for her voice, but all I could hear was the hum of the air conditioner.

I reached for the door handle and pushed it down. The door clicked open.

I jumped at the sight of Bettina. She was standing directly on the opposite side of the door with a strange expression on her face. She seemed dazed.

"Bettina?"

She lifted her eyes and met mine. "I'm scared for you," she said.

"Why would you say that?" I asked.

"Because of what you're going to find out today," she continued. She held out her hand. In it was a slip of paper with numbers and letters scrawled on it in pencil. "Here."

I hesitated for a second before taking the piece of paper from her. "What's this?"

She took a step back and almost collided with a spinning rack of sunglasses. "It's where you'll find the answers," she said. "It's an address."

I glanced down at the paper in my hand. "I can see that."

"Go there," she said, "so you'll know."

"So I'll know about what?" I prompted.

"The boy you fell in love with last night," she said. "Dominic. The truth about him."

"What are you talking about?" I asked. "Bettina, tell me."

Bettina and I were both surprised when the glass door of the boutique flew open. I felt a blast of hot, humid air from the sun-drenched street. We turned toward the entrance of the store in time to see Topher rush inside, breathless, sweaty, and wide-eyed.

"Your…brother," he panted.

Bettina shook off whatever had a momentary hold on her and her bitter persona returned. "Are you serious?" she said. "Doesn't he have anything else better to do?"

I gestured toward the door. "Maybe you should ask him yourself," I said. A tall, lanky boy with curly blond hair and an acne-covered forehead entered the boutique. "I'm assuming that's Boyd."

Bettina moved toward her younger brother. "What's your problem, Boyd? Why do ya keep messin' with him?"

"Mind your own business, Bettina."

"You're in my store," she reminded him. "Now it's my business."

"Tell him to come outside with me, then," Boyd said to his sister.

"Tell him yourself," she replied.

Boyd moved toward Topher. I stepped between them.

"Who are *you*?" Boyd asked.

I stared him in the eye. "I'm Destiny."

I felt his gaze creep all over my body. "You're kinda hot." He leered at me.

"You're kinda not," I replied.

He smiled at me, revealing a mouth of metal. Braces? Zits? A bad haircut? And no sense of style? *This* was one of Topher's tormentors?

He inched closer to me. "Why don'tcha gimme your number, Destiny?"

I held my hand up, indicating if he took a step closer I'd punch him in the face. "For many reasons you are too dumb to understand, Boyd," I said, "But mostly because I'm Topher's girlfriend."

He blinked like he'd been hit with a ball. "You're what?"

"I just moved here. From Chicago," I explained, making the story up as I went along. "We met online. We've been doing the long-distance thing, but I couldn't take it anymore. I had to be with Topher. So I convinced my dad to let me move here."

"Wait," Boyd said, "You're with...*him*?"

"For seven months now," I lied.

"That don't make no sense," he said. "Because he's a—"

"Total hottie," I completed. "I mean, just look at him. Topher is the hottest guy I've ever met. I still can't believe he likes me. Really, Boyd, I'm the luckiest girl in the world."

Boyd's lizard-like eyes darted back and forth between Topher and me. "If you say so," he decided.

Bettina was staring at me in open-mouthed disbelief.

Topher kept his eyes to the ground.

Boyd continued checking me out, even though I'd made it clear he didn't stand a chance in hell.

I handed Bettina the cash my uncle had given me. "Can you wrap the dress up for me?" I asked. "I have somewhere else to go."

My voice brought her back to the here and now. "Yeah," she said, "sure thing, love child."

Topher lifted his beautiful eyes and took a bold step forward. He shook his head. "I can't let you do this, Destiny."

"Topher," I cautioned. "Don't."

"Boyd," he said with firmness. "Destiny is *not* my girlfriend."

Boyd didn't waste any time. "Look, man, if you're breaking up with her, do you mind if I go for it?" he asked. "I think I might have a shot, bro."

I almost threw up in my mouth. Just the thought of Boyd touching me...*and he has dirty fingernails. Gross.*

Topher's voice wavered. He was nervous, scared, but brave. "She's never been my girlfriend, but she *is* one of my best friends."

I am? That's so sweet. Topher, I wanna hug you.

Boyd looked at me, wounded. "You lied to me."

"I didn't have a choice," I said. "You and your friends are jerks to him."

Topher held Boyd's stare. "I'm gay, Boyd. I don't like girls. I never have. I never will."

Boyd was blindsided. "What the…?"

"So if you want to hit me, go ahead," Topher said. "You and Skeeter and Nathan can beat me up every day, but it won't change anything. I'm still gonna be *me*."

❖

"You said that to him?" Tasha asked a few minutes later. Topher nodded eagerly in response. The big smile on his face was contagious. He seemed liberated. Empowered. Like he could start the entire world on fire. "I don't believe it."

"It's true," I said. "I was there. I saw the whole thing."

"Of course I had to miss it," Tasha said. "You finally stand up to one of those Neanderthals and I'm not there to witness it because my stupid mother made me take her to the nail salon. That woman needs a driver's license once and for all, I swear."

"I couldn't let Destiny lie," Topher explained. "She told Boyd she was my girlfriend. I think he bought it, too. Until I told him the truth."

"And then what did he do?" Tasha said, hanging on Topher's every word.

"He gave me this really weird look and said *All right, bro. Later then.* And then he just walked out the door."

Tasha was confused. "That's it? No violence? No bloodshed?"

"Easy, Tasha. You almost sound disappointed I'm still in one piece." Topher made a face at her.

"No, I'm happy you're okay," she said. "Do you think it's over now? Do you think they'll still chase you?"

Topher was sitting next to me, so I could feel his body relax a little "I hope not," he said. "And if they do, I'm not gonna let it happen anymore."

"What do you mean?" I asked.

He turned to me and said, "I'm tired of running, Destiny. If I don't move, they can't chase me."

The three of us were crammed together, shoulder to shoulder, in the cab of Tasha's stepfather's filthy pickup. Tasha had mentioned we were heading north toward Charleston, cruising there on a two-lane highway. We had the windows rolled down because the air conditioner was busted. The August afternoon wind rushing in and around us wasn't cool enough against my skin. My entire body felt hot, swollen. I pushed my hair out of my face. *Of all days to wear it down, I picked this one.*

Topher was holding his cell phone, carefully watching a GPS app he was using to guide us to our destination.

"Take the next left," he said. "There should be a church on one corner and a gas station on the other."

"Um…this is South Carolina," Tasha reminded us. "Isn't there a church on *every* corner in this state?"

"Are we already there?" I asked, feeling a wave of nerves suddenly rise in my stomach. "So soon?"

"Just a coupla more miles," Topher said. I could hear the anxiety in his words. Both of my new friends were just as excited as I was at the possibility of Dominic and me coming face-to-face for a second time. We'd mutually agreed that after our unannounced visit to his house, we'd set out on a quest to find Juliet for Tasha and Pablo for Topher. Maybe once the six of us were reunited, we could triple date. We would become a family of our own. I already had visions of movie nights, pizza parlors, road trips, beach bonfires, and all-night heart-to-heart talks.

Maybe living in Avalon Cove won't be so bad after all. Maybe I'll stop missing Chicago so much. Crap! I need to call Samantha soon. Make sure she's still alive.

"This is kinda far for Dominic to go all the way to Avalon Cove for school," Tasha said. "Maybe he's homeschooled. I hope he has a car."

"I'm sure he does," I said. "If not…there's always the weekends."

"What are you gonna say when you see him?" Topher asked.

"I wanna start with *hello*," I decided. "*Marry me* seems a little forward."

Topher's shoulders tensed. "This is it. Turn here," he directed Tasha.

We turned off the main highway and onto a graveled road lined on both sides with tall pine trees. About a half a mile later, the road opened up to a simple-looking two-story house with a beautiful wooden wraparound porch. The house was mostly brick, but the trim around the windows was wooden, painted white. There was a tire swing in the front yard, hanging down from the thick limb of an enormous tree. The entire house was surrounded by purple and yellow wildflowers.

Tasha stopped the truck and turned off the engine. We stared through the windshield. "Your new boyfriend lives in the country," she said. "We're nowhere near the beach."

"I thought Avalon Cove was small," Topher said. "But this feels like we're in the middle of nowhere."

"Dominic can't help it," I said, in his defense. "Maybe his father is a farmer. Or maybe he's the sheriff or something like that."

"You've been watching too many movies," Tasha said.

"Or not enough," Topher added.

I reached for the metal door handle and pulled it open. I stepped out of the truck and reached toward the graveled ground with the tip of my sandal.

My mouth was dry. My palms were sweaty. I moved toward the house with caution, still unsure of what I would say to Dominic once we were face-to-face.

Should I hug him? Shake his hand? Make out with him on the tire swing?

I looked up. The screen door creaked open. I froze in my tracks. A tall, thin woman stood in the doorway. I could tell she'd once been really beautiful, but life had been unkind and taken a toll on her. Her honey-colored hair was pulled back but loose strands hung around her face. She was wearing a dark pink short-sleeved blouse, a pair of Capri blue jeans, and white flip-flops. I could tell she was older than us, but she looked too young to be someone's mother.

"Can I help you?" she said. Her voice was sweet and welcoming. I moved closer.

She's probably his older sister. That means if things go the way I'm hoping they do, she could one day be my sister-in-law.

I realized I hadn't planned on what I'd say if Dominic wasn't home. The woman was staring at me, like she was waiting for me to say something.

First impressions are so important, Destiny. Remember your manners.

"I'm sorry to bother you," I began. "I'm a…friend…of Dominic's. I came by to see him. Is he home?"

She took a slow, heavy step onto the porch. And another. The screen door slammed shut behind her. The gunshot-like noise made me jump but she didn't even flinch. I glanced back nervously to my friends in the truck, contemplating running back to them and telling Tasha to floor it all the way back to Avalon Cove.

As the woman came closer, I couldn't stop staring into her eyes. They reminded me of Dominic's—the same light shade of hazel.

"You know my son?" she said.

Your son? Were you twelve when you had him?

I nodded. "Yes. My name is Destiny Moore. He's not expecting me. I didn't have his cell number. Otherwise I would've called. I'm very sorry to just show up... unannounced."

Tears suddenly flooded her eyes. It unnerved me. It made me want to leave immediately. But I also felt compelled to go to her, embrace her, and tell her everything was going to be okay. Something was obviously wrong. Something really terrible had happened.

She sat down on the top step and wiped her face. I noticed her hands were trembling.

"I'm sorry," I said. "Did I say something wrong? I can go. We can leave."

She shook her head and struggled to regain her composure. "Come," she said. She gestured to the empty space beside her by patting the wood beneath her. "Sit with me for a minute. Then you can be on your way."

I obliged, moving cautiously up the steps to the porch. I sat down beside her.

"You seem like a real sweet girl," she said. A tear slid down her cheek. She brushed it away with the back of her hand. "That's why it's real hard for me to tell you what I gotta say. I don't know you, so I'm not sure how you're gonna take it. I don't know if you've ever lost somebody before."

She fell silent for a moment. I wondered if she was searching for the right words.

Finally, I spoke, just to fill the space between us. "I feel awful," I said. "I shouldn't have bothered you. I have no right just showing up like this. Me and my friends didn't know better. Honest."

I stood up to leave but she reached out and touched my arm. She guided me gently back down to the wooden steps.

"I'm not sure how long it's been since you've seen my son," she said, "but I need to let you know…" She stopped for a moment, overwhelmed by her emotions. It was difficult for her to get the words out. "Dominic…he ain't here."

I swallowed, fearing the worst. "Where is he?" I asked.

She reached for my hand and squeezed it. "Honey, he died," she said. "My beautiful boy's been dead for five weeks."

CHAPTER NINE

It took a second for the words to sink in. I couldn't process them right away. They were too heavy and cruel. More important, they didn't make any sense to me.

I thought about turning to Dominic's mother and insisting she was wrong. *What you're saying to me can't possibly be true. I was with your son last night. He's beautiful and romantic. When I was a little girl, I dreamed of marrying a boy just like him one day. We danced together. And I think we fell in love. I'm pretty sure I want to spend the rest of my life with him. But how can I? Take those awful words back. Please.*

Instead, I pulled my hand away from hers as if I'd been wounded or burned. I stared down at my palms, at the lines and patterns on my skin. "Dominic is dead?" I asked.

She nodded, still crying. "I know it's not easy to hear," she said. "He was a wonderful son. A real good person. He took care of us. He worked real hard. Never complained about nothing. He was the best thing that ever happened to me. I swear to you."

Was he? I'll never get the chance to find out for myself.

"I believe you," I said. "But I don't understand how he can be dead...when he made me feel so alive."

"Destiny," his mother said, "may I ask you a rather personal question?" I nodded, giving her permission. "Were you and my son only *friends*...or were the two of you something more?"

I glanced out to the pickup truck. Tasha and Topher were out of earshot, but they were watching my every move, waiting. I knew they were hoping Dominic would appear at any second and they could watch our reunion, like something out of a movie. Later, they were hoping for similar moments to occur with Juliet and Pablo.

And then it hit me.

If Dominic was dead, Juliet and Pablo probably were as well.

We've fallen in love with ghosts.

The purpose of Wonderland—and the reason Tasha, Topher, and I had been invited there—was becoming clearer to me by the second. In my mind, I started to replay all of my conversations with Adrianna.

This is my moment to do something for you. To give you a chance at true love.

What exactly was she offering us? A love affair with someone who'd already died? Why?

I tried to piece it together in my mind—the truth about Wonderland. Somehow people who had recently died ended up there. My great-aunt played matchmaker by inviting people who were alive to a dinner party they'd never forget. Adrianna took it upon herself to make the initial introductions. But now what? Sometime soon, I'd be given a choice, most likely to change the fate of someone and bring them back.

From the dead.

"How did he die?" I asked.

"A car accident," she explained. "Head-on collision with a tree. He was trying to take a shortcut not far from here. Made it halfway across the field before he lost control of the car."

"Lost control?" I repeated.

"It was raining real bad that night," she said, "and he was in an awful hurry."

"A hurry to get where?"

"To the hospital."

"To see you?" I asked.

"No," a throaty voice said from behind us. We both turned in unison toward the screen door. An older woman with a round face was standing in the doorway of the house with one hand across her heart as if she were pledging her allegiance to something or someone. She was solid and broad and looked tough. I assumed she was Native American. Her thick black hair was parted in the middle and pulled back into a long braid. She was wearing a pair of old blue jeans, a baggy black T-shirt, and a pair of tattered sneakers. "He was coming to see me," she explained. "He was on his way to the hospital when the accident happened."

She moved toward us. Before I realized it, she was sitting next to me. I was bookended by two brokenhearted women who clearly loved Dominic very much. Their sorrow felt suffocating. It permeated the air. I felt like all sense of hope and happiness was being choked out of me. I covered my mouth, coughed.

"This here's Valerie." The older woman's voice was commanding, but her words were weighed down with a sense of sadness that sounded permanent. It was a chore just for her to speak. "You can call me Mama June."

"Mama June," I repeated. *I like that.* "It's nice to meet you. I'm Destiny."

"Yeah, I know," she said. "I had a…feeling you were coming to see us today."

Does everyone in South Carolina have the ability to see into the future? Maybe she's a distant cousin of Bettina's.

"How did you know Dominic?" I asked.

She gave a nervous glance to Valerie, took a breath, and

said, "Dominic was Valerie's biological son, but we both raised him."

"Oh," I said, not really understanding what she meant. Were they sisters? Was this woman a nanny of some kind? A neighbor who lent a helping hand?

She could tell I was clueless. "He had two moms," she clarified for me. "Val and I have been together for over fifteen years."

I turned to Valerie, and back to Mama June.

Oh, I get it now.

"Well, he was very lucky, then," I said. "I only had one mom. And she's gone now."

Valerie lifted her eyes up to the summer sky and said, "I wonder if your mother knows my son."

I nodded, blinking back tears. "I'm sure she does."

"We weren't a typical family but we loved Dominic very much," Mama June said. "He was everything to us."

"I'm so sorry…for your loss," I said. "I know what it feels like to lose someone you love."

"We never expected something like this to happen," Valerie explained. "Not to him. My boy was so young."

"Nothing for us will ever be the same," Mama June told me. Her voice cracked with heavy emotions. "We're not sure what to do now."

"Do you get to Avalon Cove very often?" I asked.

"Not as much as we used to," Valerie said. "We used to take Dominic there when he was little, to the beach. He loved the water. I bought him this sketchbook once. He used to sit there in the sand painting and drawing little pictures of the sailboats in the harbor. Sometimes we'd take him to the playground there. Or have a picnic lunch in the park. Those were good times."

"It's a nice place," Mama June said, "but it's a little too busy for our taste. We're country girls at heart. We're happy here in Harmonville."

"I have two uncles," I said, blurting the words out. "They've been together for years. They love each other a whole lot. I live with them now. My mom gave them legal guardianship. So…we're a family, too."

"Wow," Valerie said with a faint smile, "you and Dominic had a lot in common."

Did we? Or, do we? We've spent all of five minutes together. I know next to nothing about him. And now I want to know even more.

"We hadn't known each other for very long," I said. "So, there's still a lot I don't know about Dominic. But we definitely had a connection."

"I have no manners," Valerie said, standing up. "Would you and your friends like to come inside? I just made some iced tea. You could come in…and cool off…and talk. I have some photo albums if you wanna see 'em."

I was tempted. I wanted nothing more than to delve deeper into Dominic's world. I wanted to see where he grew up, the table he ate dinner at with this two moms, the bed he slept in, the grade school photos, all the other one-of-a-kind things that had made him who he had been.

I looked to Tasha and Topher, who appeared to be melting inside the truck. They would've appreciated something cool to drink, but I had to tell them the truth about Juliet and Pablo. I owed it to them. And the sooner, the better.

I tried to ignore the hope in Valerie's gentle eyes. I was a connection to her lost son. It was clear she didn't want me to leave.

We'll swing through a drive-thru on the way back to

the island and get something to drink. I can come back here another time. Right now, it's really important to tell your new BFF's that our soul mates are no longer living.

"That's very sweet," I said to Valerie, "but we have to get back on the road soon. I have to go back to work. My uncles are probably wondering where I am."

"Maybe you'll come back then…another time?" Valerie said, holding my gaze.

"She will," Mama June assured us both. She shifted her attention solely to me. "I want you to know something."

I waited for her to continue, hoping she was going to tell me this entire scenario was one big cruel joke—and then Dominic would burst out of the house, bound down the steps, and throw his arms around me, declaring to the world, *This is the woman of my dreams.* He would spin us around in a grand, sweeping circle and my feet would be lifted off the ground. I would feel weightless and breathless. Mama June and Valerie would watch us with love shining in their eyes, for each other and for the fact they knew Dominic and I would be together forever.

We'd go inside. Valerie would make us something to eat. Mama June would share funny stories about the crazy things Dominic did as a child. He and I would sit together, hold hands, occasionally look into each other's eyes. Later, the four of us would sit around the dinner table. We would laugh until we cried. We would be a family. And we would be happy.

"Dominic died trying to get to me," Mama June said. She lowered her dark eyes to the cracked and peeling floor of the porch. "Doctors said there was no hope for me. I wasn't going to make it. Stage 4 cancer. Inoperable. That's what they said."

"It's true," Valerie echoed. "And it happened so fast. It was just a matter of weeks."

"It's real hard for me not to feel responsible," Mama June said.

"You know it's not your fault," Valerie reminded her. "You can't keep blaming yourself. It was an accident."

"If I wouldn't have gotten sick…"

"I called Dominic because the doctors told me to. They said there wasn't much more time," Valerie explained. "I knew he'd want to be with his Mama June. He was crazy about her."

"He was racing to be by my side," Mama June said. "Because that's the kind of man he was. But it was starting to rain. So he decided to cut through the field to save some time."

"Around the same time Dominic collided with the tree, my beautiful June regained consciousness."

"The newspaper called it a miracle," Mama June said. "Even the doctors couldn't figure it out. They said I was lucky. They said I beat the odds. I thought I had. I asked where my boy was because it seemed strange he wasn't there. And that's when the lady deputy came into the hospital room to tell us what happened to Dominic."

"Do you believe it was a miracle?" I asked. "That you survived?"

Mama June shook her head. "I believe it was magic," she said. "I believe Dominic must've made a deal with God."

Or with my great-aunt Adrianna. Somehow he found his way to Wonderland and saved his Mama June.

"No one can tell me how I survived," she said. "A full recovery. I'm cancer-free."

"My mother died of cancer," I said. "Two weeks ago. It happened really fast. I was busy with school and stuff when she first got sick. I guess maybe I didn't pay much attention to what was going on with her because a part of me believed she would get better…but…she didn't."

"I'm very sorry to hear that," Mama June said. "I'm sure she was a fine lady."

"Yes, she was," I said. "Maybe I didn't realize it before this…before she died."

I stood up. I walked down the steps and returned to the graveled road. I turned back to my new friends on the porch. "My mother was a dancer," I said. "And she was beautiful. She grew up in Avalon Cove. I live there now."

"I hope you got to say good-bye," Valerie said.

"We never got that chance to tell Dominic what he meant to us," Mama June said.

Don't worry. I'll figure out a way to bring him back home.

❖

I didn't know what to say to Tasha or Topher moments later when I climbed back into the old pickup truck. I avoided their curious eyes. "Let's go," were the only words I could get out.

Tasha waited until we were back on the two-lane highway before she asked me, "So, what happened? We couldn't hear a thing."

"It wasn't what I expected," I replied.

"That bad?" Tasha said. "Does he have a wife and kids?"

"No," I said, "but he has two moms who loved him very much."

"Two moms?" Topher repeated. "That's so cool."

"Yeah, how come I didn't get two moms?" Tasha said with a grin. "Or two uncles? I feel cheated."

"Are you gonna see him again?" Topher asked. "Did you leave a number so he can call you? Maybe he can come and meet us somewhere."

"I have a feeling he'll be at Wonderland," I said. "And so will Juliet and Pablo. Something tells me we'll each be seeing them again soon."

Tasha tightened her grip on the steering wheel. "What makes you so sure?"

"Let's go to the playground and I'll tell you," I suggested.

Tasha shook her head. "No, thank you. It's a hundred degrees outside."

"Yeah, it's too hot for the playground," Topher agreed.

"Then let's find a place with some air-conditioning," I said. "I have to tell you guys something."

"This sounds serious," Tasha noted. "Do you have bad news or good news for us?"

"That depends," I said.

"On what?"

"On whether or not the two of you *really* believe in magic."

❖

Dominic was in my dream that night. I wasn't sure if it was him at first. I was in Chicago. It was a spring day. I was standing on an outdoor platform, waiting for an "L" train to arrive. I don't know where I was headed or why I was wearing a white cashmere sweater, a black miniskirt, and really uncomfortable high heels, but it felt like I was supposed to be there. It was where I belonged.

I took a step closer to the edge, looked both ways, but

there was no train in sight. I stepped back into the crowd of passengers. Most of them were men dressed for work in suits and ties. My eyes drifted over to the opposite platform, across the tracks.

And that's when I saw him.

He was alone, also waiting for a train. He had on blue jeans, a white tee, and a charcoal gray pea coat. He slid his hands into the pockets of the coat. Even though the sun was out, I was worried Dominic was cold.

Our eyes met. Neither one of us could look away. His mouth lifted into a beautiful smile. "Destiny?" he said just barely loud enough for me to hear him above the floating conversations of the crowd. There was a slight hint of desperation in his voice, mixed with a tinge of hope.

Maybe he's fallen in love with me, too. Maybe this dream is somehow real.

In the distance, I could see and hear Dominic's train approaching. I knew I only had a matter of seconds before he was gone. I had no choice: I had to get to him.

I turned. I ran. I pushed and shoved my way through the crowd of executives, hurried down the wooden steps to the station below, darted across to the opposite staircase, and rushed up to the platform.

Once I reached the top step, there was a sudden shift and everything began to move in slow motion, even me.

I saw him.

I saw the train arrive.

"Don't go," I pleaded. My voice was muddled.

"My train is here," he said. His words sounded like they were rolling through a tunnel to reach me.

I was trying to get to him, but there were so many people in my way. I maneuvered around them the best I could.

Finally…

I reached out to him, to touch his face.

He looked into my eyes and said, "I love you, Destiny. I've never met a girl like you, but I've always wanted to. You are, without a doubt, everything I've ever dreamed of."

With that, he turned away from me and stepped onto the train. I watched the doors close. He looked back and stared at me through the glass.

"I love you, too!" I shouted.

The train started to pull away. I ran beside it, desperate and frightened.

"Don't leave," I begged. "Dominic!"

❖

Someone was touching me. I could feel a hand on my shoulder, shaking me gently. I opened my eyes and stared up at Clark. He was standing over me with a cordless telephone in his hand.

"Destiny," he said, "I'm so sorry to wake you. Tasha's on the phone for you. She says it's important."

It took me a few seconds to comprehend what he was saying to me. The dream of Dominic had been intense. I was hot, sweaty. My heart was racing. I threw off the comforter and sat up in my bed.

What day is it? What time is it? Where am I? And why is everything still so pink?

I took the phone form Clark and said, "Thank you."

"If you're up to it, I made some coffee and some oatmeal raisin cookies. They're downstairs waiting for you," he said. "You slept through dinner. I could warm you up a plate, if you'd like."

"Sounds great," I said. "I'll be down in a sec."

I waited until Clark had pulled my bedroom door closed before I put the phone to my ear.

"Tasha?"

"It's so sad how they died," she said.

"Tasha, are you crying?" I asked. "What's the matter?"

"We found them," she said. "Topher and me. It took a while, but we finally found them."

"Juliet and Pablo? Where? Are they okay? Are they alive?"

"No," she said. "They're dead, too. Just like Dominic. You were right."

"How?" I asked.

"Pablo was a foreign exchange student from Spain. He was here for a year, living with a family in Charleston. His plane never made it back home."

"He died in a plane crash?" I said. "That's awful."

"And Juliet...she was a couple of years older than us. She already graduated from high school. She was also living in Charleston. She was a concert pianist. She had a full scholarship to Juilliard. They even wrote about her in the news. Everyone thought she was going to become famous."

"Wow," I said. "She must've been really talented."

"She was," Tasha said. "But she died trying to save a little boy who couldn't swim. She worked as a camp counselor during the summers. I guess he fell into the water somehow. She went in after him. Only she wasn't strong enough to swim against the current."

"That's so sad."

"She was a hero. That's what all of the newspapers wrote about her. It's even online."

"At least you know...how it happened," I said.

"I don't get it, Destiny."

"What do you mean?" I asked.

"All three of them seem like they were really good people. They didn't do anything wrong to anyone," she said. "So why did they have to die?"

"I completely agree," I said. "I've been thinking about that since I met Dominic's moms."

"Why them? Why not the Neanderthals? No one would even miss those guys."

"Bettina might miss Boyd," I reminded her. "Since he *is* her brother."

Tasha took a deep breath before she spoke. "Topher and I've decided…when we go to Wonderland, we want to bring them back. It's the right thing to do. Who knows what Pablo and Juliet can still become…if we give 'em the chance."

"I figured that's what you guys would decide."

"I don't know how it works," she said. "But I'm sure Adrianna will explain it to us."

"I'm sure she will," I said. "And I hope it happens soon. For all of us."

"What about you?" she asked. "Are you going to bring Dominic back?"

CHAPTER TEN

A drianna looked at us from where she stood on the second to the last step of the staircase. She was wearing a pale lemon chiffon dress, gold shoes, and a diamond-studded hairpin. Her platinum hair was down, framing her face in loose curls.

"Welcome back," she said with a gentle smile.

Tasha, Topher, and I stood in the foyer of Wonderland breathless and holding hands. Just seconds ago we'd been backstage at the Magic Mansion, crammed inside a closet-sized dressing room. I was sitting at a vanity table in front of a square lit mirror, checking my reflection one last time before the show started. It was going to be my debut as Sir Frederic's assistant, and my two best friends were there to support me. Tasha was thumbing through a rack of old costumes. She discovered a black feathered boa I was certain had once belonged to my grandmother. She wrapped it around her shoulders and pranced and posed around the dressing room like a glamorous diva. Topher was sitting on the floor skimming through an Italian-English dictionary, trying his best to pronounce new words and phrases.

The round lights bordering the frame of the dressing room mirror and the bare lightbulb above our heads flickered. We raised our eyes, looking up in unison.

A smile crept across Tasha's face. "You guys," she said. "I think this is it."

The room went black. I shut my eyes. In an instant, we were off. We were flying. I could feel my body being propelled through cool air. I knew Tasha and Topher were at my sides. I reached out for them in the darkness. I found their hands and held them in mine.

I had a sense that this wild journey we'd been on for the last few days would soon be coming to an end. We were headed back to Wonderland, where we would each make a life-changing choice. Once we did, I expected our lives would return to some state of normal. I could finally focus on settling into my new life in Avalon Cove. I could devote time to getting to know my uncles better. I could really bond with Tasha and Topher. I could come up with some sure-fire strategies to keep the Magic Mansion from closing. And, maybe, if all went the way I wanted it to, I could fall deeply in love with Dominic.

"Hello, Adrianna," I said to my great-aunt.

"Is that a new dress?" she asked. "Just for this occasion?"

I glanced down at the knee-length black dress I was wearing, my costume for the magic show. "It's actually for my new job," I explained. "At the Magic Mansion."

"You're following in your grandmother's footsteps, I see," she said. "I hope you're a better assistant than she is."

"Don't count on it," I said. "But then again, I won't be making a career out of it."

"That's what she thought," my great-aunt said. "You can't avoid the magic, Destiny. It's a part of who you are."

"It's my legacy," I said. "I know. And I've accepted that. I just don't understand why."

"Because I can't do this forever," she said. "As much as I want to."

I almost laughed. "It seems like you call all the shots around here."

"That's where you're wrong," she said. "I was chosen once, too. Just like all of you."

"By my grandfather?" I asked. "He's really the one behind all of this, isn't he?"

"My brother is a brilliant man. He was terribly misunderstood by most people who met him in your world, but he was very, very smart," she explained. "He saw something in you. He called it pure magic. Maybe it's because you have such a big heart. You really do care about the people in your life. You love them with everything you have."

"I do," I said. "Including you."

"Truthfully, I see a lot of myself in you. In due time you'll grow to realize all that's been given to you by your ancestors. The possibilities. The power. I know you will only use it for good."

"Always," I promised.

Adrianna moved down to the last step of the stairs. "I know the three of you are anxious to be reunited with Dominic and Juliet and Pablo. And I know how desperately they each want to see the three of you."

"Are they here?" Topher asked, barely able to contain his excitement. He hadn't stopped grinning since we arrived.

"Not so fast," Adrianna cautioned. "There's a lot to tell you first."

"Adrianna, I understand why you chose Destiny to be here," Tasha said. "She's your niece. It makes sense. But why did you include me and Topher? I mean, we're just the kids at school no one talks to."

"I did it to bond the three of you together," she said. "Individually, you each represent hope and faith and love. Each of you is ruled by those three virtues. Every choice you make is based on your belief in them. Collectively, I think you make a beautiful family. There's no biological connection between the three of you, but DNA doesn't always equal a wonderful family life. More and more, the opposite is true. To me, you've become a family of your own. I brought you here to experience something that would seal your friendship forever. If any of you doubted Wonderland for a second, this wouldn't work. I had to make sure you each believed before I could allow you to proceed."

"So, does this mean we passed?" Topher asked.

She reached out and placed a gentle palm against his cheek. "With flying colors."

"Have there been others like us? Other friends?" I asked.

She shook her head. "No. Not as many as you would think. True friendship is almost as rare as true love. Both are very hard to find. But both are worth fighting for."

"And dying for?" I said.

"Have you figured out the method to my madness?" she asked.

"I think I just did," I said. "You really are a matchmaker, in more ways than one. When my mother got sick and she knew she was going to die, she decided to send me here—to live in Avalon Cove. She knew I would eventually find my way to Wonderland. She knew about this place. She knew it existed and what it was about."

"Yes," Adrianna agreed. "Of course."

"You made sure I met Tasha and Topher. You knew they would bring me here."

"Indeed I did."

"And the beautiful people you chose for us to fall in love with—you knew they would be perfect for us. Each of them died a very noble death."

Adrianna thought about it for a moment. "For the most part...yes."

"Just like when my Uncle Fred came to you and asked you to bring back Clark."

"I couldn't deny his request," she explained. "Those men are deeply in love and always will be."

"So you've spent the last decade living in this house doing good deeds for people?"

"Not exactly," she said. "It's not quite that simple. There's a process."

"What? Like an application?" Topher asked.

"Not so formal," she answered. "But the selection criteria are quite considerable. Very few people are ever invited to Wonderland. And even fewer make it to this very point where the three of you are. I wouldn't say it's impossible to do, but you need to know that what you're about to experience truly is the opportunity of a lifetime. I don't make this happen for just anybody."

"I feel like we need to thank you," Tasha said. "You've done more for me than anyone."

"Except for maybe Sir Frederic the Great," Topher chimed in. "And Clark."

"I appreciate your gratitude, but I don't do any of this for acknowledgment," my great-aunt said.

"Why do you do it then?" I asked.

"Simple," she said. "I do this for love."

I took a step in her direction and said, "I know this is my legacy. I know my grandfather selected me and that you agree with him. I realize that one day Wonderland and the Magic Mansion will become mine. But you have to know something...I will never be able to be you."

"I would never ask that of you," she said. "Wonderland

will be very different under your care. I expect many changes will occur. But I know you. I know what's in your heart. You will always be ruled by love. Just like me."

"How does it work?" Tasha asked. "What happens next? Do we go back into the courtyard? Do they get to come home with us?"

"Not quite," Adrianna said. "Each of you will go back to the deciding moment. To the very second when Dominic and Juliet and Pablo made the choice that ultimately led to their deaths. They will not be able to see you or hear you, but they will be able to sense your energy. Your presence. The moment will be very real for them. And for you. You will experience it just as they did before. It will be up to you to change their minds, which will eventually change their fates."

"Isn't it wrong to do that?" I asked. "As much as I love Dominic, what if this was his time to go?"

"But it wasn't," she said.

I gave her a look, hoping she would explain further. "I don't understand."

"It was Mama June's time to go."

"What?" I heard myself say.

"Dominic made the ultimate sacrifice."

I felt tears fill the corners of my eyes. "He did that?"

"Yes," she said. "Without hesitation."

"He gave up his own life?"

"Actually," Adrianna said, "they all did. Otherwise they'd never have been invited to Wonderland. The rules are very specific."

"The little boy who fell in the water at the summer camp? The one Juliet jumped in to save?" Tasha said. "What really happened to him?"

"He didn't survive initially," Adrianna explained. "Juliet knew the boy's family very well. Their oldest son was a soldier who had been killed overseas just a few years prior. She couldn't stand to see them brokenhearted again. She, too, made a sacrifice."

"And Pablo?" Topher said. "There were no survivors. Everyone on the plane died."

"Except for the flight attendant whose alarm clock didn't go off that morning. She missed the plane and was almost fired for doing so. Last week, while she was walking through the airport in Barcelona, she discovered a woman who was having a heart attack. You might meet this very lucky woman one day, Topher, since she's Pablo's mother. She says she will always be grateful to the flight attendant who truly saved her life."

I looked deep into Adrianna's green eyes. "What about my mother?" I said. "She's here at Wonderland, isn't she?"

"Of course she is," my great-aunt said with a smile. "And Clark wouldn't be alive today without her."

I took a deep breath and swallowed the waves of emotion stirring inside me. "My mother made the sacrifice?"

"She said she's never seen your uncle happier. She also knew you would be in good hands, Destiny. She knew you might even learn a thing or two about magic."

"So now it's up to us?" Tasha said. "We go back to the deciding moment and stop it from happening?"

"If that's your choice, yes."

"And then what happens?" Topher asked.

"You wait," Adrianna answered. "And you see."

"How long do we have with them?" I asked.

"As long as it takes," she replied. "I'll know when to bring you out."

"When they come back, will they know us?" I asked.

"Yes," she said. "And they'll know what you've done for them."

"What about the people they saved?" Tasha asked. "Will they die?"

"No," she said. "Their fate cannot be undone."

"Then let's do this," Tasha urged.

"Very well," Adrianna said. "Follow me."

We obeyed her command. We moved quickly as she led us through the front of the house, through the twisting maze of corridors and flickering sconces, into the old-fashioned kitchen, and finally to the closed door in the corner of the moonlit room.

"Tasha, you'll be first," Adrianna announced.

Tasha took a step forward. She pushed her yellow headband back to keep her hair out of her feline eyes. "Okay."

"I'm sending you to summer camp," Adrianna explained. "Remember that no one can see you or hear you. But Juliet will sense you are there."

"How much time do I have? To convince her not to jump into the water?" Tasha asked.

"Not much. You'll have to act fast. The little boy is already standing on the edge of the river. He'll make his own way back to shore."

"Got it."

Adrianna opened the door. Tasha stepped inside, into the sea of total darkness. Quickly, my great-aunt closed the door again.

"Are you ready, Topher?" she asked.

"I guess so," he said.

"You're going to the airport in Atlanta," she said. "You will only have a few moments to keep Pablo from getting on that plane to Rome."

"I'll do whatever it takes," he vowed.

"I know you will," she said. "It's my hope once you and

Pablo are together in the real world, you won't feel as alone as you do now."

Topher nodded. Then he started to cry. I felt my heart ache for him. "I hate it."

"I know you do," she said. "And so does Pablo. Never again will either of you ever be alone or scared or feel unwanted or unloved. Because you will always have each other. I've seen to it that Pablo will receive a student visa to study his art at a college in America. In fact, it's the same college you'll be studying at as well. Later, Pablo will become quite successful. His citizenship will never be a concern—as it shouldn't be."

Topher reached out and slid his arms around Adrianna, embracing her. "I don't know how I'll ever be able to thank you."

She opened the door and said, "You just did."

Topher stepped into the pitch black space. He glanced back at me and whispered, "I'll see you soon, Destiny."

My great-aunt closed the door behind him.

I took a deep breath. "I guess I'm next?" I said.

"Your situation is slightly different," she said.

An intense nervousness started to gnaw at me. "What do you mean?"

"You have a choice to make."

"I thought I already made it," I said. "I'm here. I know I want to go back and save Dominic. I have no doubt about that."

"There are other circumstances," she said.

Of course there are.

"Tell me," I prompted.

Adrianna took a breath and reached for my hands. "Your mother," she said. "You have the chance to bring her back."

My heart was racing. "Wait…I can bring them *both* back?"

My great-aunt shook her head. "No," she said. "Only one."

I pulled my hands away from her. "Are you kidding me with this?"

"I'm afraid not."

"So you're telling me I have to choose between my mother and Dominic? How is that even fair?"

"According to your mother, she knows what you'll do. She knows what your choice will be," Adrianna said.

I flashed back to the night in the courtyard when I was dancing with Dominic at the dinner party. I remembered my mother's words floating in my ear. *I want you to choose love.*

I will.

I didn't even realize I was crying until I felt tears sliding down my face. "You can't ask me to make this kind of choice, Adrianna. She's my mother."

"And what would it mean to bring her back, Destiny? What would her life be like?"

"I don't know," I said.

"Yes, you do."

"My brother and I love her very much."

"And she knows that. But your life is in Avalon Cove now. And Ian is very happy in California with Aunt Barbara."

"She was very sad," I admitted. "My mother had a broken heart. Because of my father."

"Was she a happy woman?"

"Sometimes," I said. "I think my brother and I made her happy. And whenever she danced around our living room, it seemed like she was glowing."

"She's still dancing," Adrianna assured me.

"Are you telling me to choose Dominic?" I asked.

"I can't make that decision for you," she said. "It has to be yours alone."

"How can I do this? You're asking me to choose between the woman who gave birth to me and raised me and took care of me and loved me and a man I've only spent five minutes with."

"Does that mean you would like to choose your mother?" she asked.

"No," I said. "I don't know."

"Yes, you do."

"She used to cry at night."

"I know."

"I could hear her crying through my bedroom wall. She thought I was asleep."

"She doesn't cry anymore."

"I wanted to take away her pain. Even when she was sick. Even when she was dying. I looked at her in that hospital bed and I secretly wished it was me. At the funeral, all I wanted to do was trade places with her."

"Your mother made a choice. Full recovery or bring Clark back. You know what her decision was."

"I do," I said. "She chose love."

"Wouldn't she want you to do the same?"

I closed my eyes for a moment. I saw my mother in her rose-colored skirt, peasant blouse, and jazz shoes. I could hear the haunting melody of Beethoven's *Moonlight Sonata*. She was in our living room in our apartment in Chicago, gliding across the shiny wooden floors, dancing as if no one were watching. She was lost in her movements, oblivious to the world around her, to the snow falling outside and the radiator in the corner wheezing and rumbling. She was at peace.

This is how I always want to remember you.

I knew my mother still loved my father up until the

moment she died. He really was the love of her life. Yet, he was never able to reciprocate that love on the same level. He'd never quite figured out a way to love her enough. Instead, he disappointed her time and time again. He broke her heart into a million pieces. He left her and embarked on a new life with new women. But none of them would be my mother. They wouldn't have her softness or her grace.

They wouldn't be magic.

I opened my eyes.

"I've made my decision," I said. "I choose love."

CHAPTER ELEVEN

When I opened my eyes, the first thing I saw was the silver car. The mouth of it was rammed up to the trunk of the tree, smashed against the charred bark. Smoke was spewing out from underneath the hood. The car horn was screeching and constant, echoing across the field. I was standing in the middle of what seemed to be a vegetable garden made up of endless mounded rows of green leaves poking up out of the ground. The car and the tree were at least fifty feet away from me, if not farther.

I knew I had to move quickly. My high heels kept sinking into the soft dirt, slowing me down as I hurried to reach the car.

The massive tree was naked and loomed like an ominous creature, ready to devour anyone or anything that came within its vicinity. Its branches were jagged and sharp, like angry dark arms sprawled against the overcast sky.

Lightning flashed and illuminated the field with a burst of stark white. Thunder followed, and the roar of it terrified me. Heavy rain began to fall. Within seconds I was drenched to the bone. I pushed my wet hair out of my eyes once I finally reached the car.

There were puddles of shattered glass everywhere. My high heels crunched against it with each careful step I took.

I could see Dominic through the driver's side window. He was slumped over the steering wheel, unconscious.

"Dominic," I said, overwhelmed by the sight of him.

No one can hear you in this universe, Destiny.

I pulled on the door handle, but the car door was jammed. It wouldn't open. I moved around to the passenger side. The passenger door opened without much effort. I leaned down and reached into the car, my fingertips extended toward Dominic.

You can't touch him. He won't feel it.

I tried anyway. In the sliver of the second that my hand was to make contact with his body, something happened. The entire world seemed to shift into reverse. I slid into the passenger seat just as the car pulled back away from the tree. The damage to the car disappeared. We were moving backward. It was as if we were stuck in rewind mode at the hands of someone pushing a button on a remote control.

I heard nothing but silence, a complete audio void. Not even the sound of my own heart beating. Or my breath.

We were moving faster now, still going backward. The threatening tree grew smaller in the distance. The field soon became a blur of green leaves and dirt.

And then we stopped.

I looked through the windshield. We were idling at a four-way stop, at a rural intersection. Nothing but vast farmland surrounded us. Rain was pounding hard against the car. The flimsy windshield wipers on the compact vehicle could barely keep up.

I saw the contemplation in Dominic's eyes.

He's going to take the shortcut. He's going to cut through the field. This is his deciding moment. Do something, Destiny. Now.

I heard Dominic's voice. "I'll be there as soon as I can," he said. It took me a second to realize he was talking to someone on his cell phone. I stared at him. The sight of his profile caused the air to catch in my lungs. He took my breath away. He was wearing a pair of old jeans and a green T-shirt that was on inside out. His thick brown hair was a mess. It was obvious he'd gotten dressed in a hurry, in a moment of complete panic. "She has to hold on until I get there," he said.

I felt my heart break when Dominic started to cry. He clutched the steering wheel until his knuckles paled. "It's not fair, Mom," he sobbed. "She's never done anything wrong to anybody. She doesn't deserve this."

Even though he couldn't hear me, I had to say something. "She's gonna be okay. I promise."

Dominic's cries grew more intense. "What are we gonna do without her?"

I reached for him on instinct. Then I remembered.

Feel my presence, Dominic. I'm here. I chose you. I chose love.

"She'll make a full recovery," I said. "She's cancer free. She's waiting for you at home. She needs you, Dominic. So does your mom. So do I."

Dominic's sobs subsided for a moment. A strange expression crept over his face. "Mom, did you say something?"

"She told you to turn around," I said. "She said to go back home, Dominic. Listen to your mother."

"Mom?"

"Do what she tells you!"

"Mom, can you hear me?"

"Turn the car around. Please."

"Mom?" he said. "Oh, there you are. I thought I lost you."

"I can't lose you, Dominic. Not after what we've gone through to be together," I said. "My great-aunt says we were meant for each other. We're soul mates. You're perfect for me. And I want to be perfect for you. But you can't go into that field. You'll lose control of the car."

"Mom, I'm gonna take a shortcut."

"No!" I said as loud as I could. "You can't."

"I'm gonna cut through the field. I'll be there in like two minutes."

"Don't do it," I pleaded. "Turn the car around. Take a different route."

"I love you, too," he said. His voice started to break again as his sorrow resurfaced. His pushed a button on his cell phone before it slipped from his hand and landed on the floor of the car right between my mud-caked black high heels.

Dominic hit the accelerator. We slid off the asphalt andskidded onto the dirt as we entered the field. The tree was just up ahead, waiting.

It's now or never, Destiny.

"Dominic, I know you can't hear me or see me, but I know you can feel my presence. You know you're not alone right now. I can see it in your eyes. I love you very much. I want to spend the rest of my life with you. And then after that we can live at Wonderland and make other people just as happy as we are. I need you to stop this car. I need you to put your foot on the brake now. Turn the car around. Go a different way. Mama June is going to be fine. Do you hear me?"

Dominic glanced in my direction. For a moment I thought we made eye contact.

He knows you're here.

I stared through the windshield. The rain was relentless. It was difficult to see. I could make out the gnarled branches and the black limbs of the evil tree. We were getting closer to it. It was only a matter of seconds.

"Dominic, please," I begged. "Stop the car!"

Instead, he started to speed up. I could see the heavy sadness in his eyes. On instinct, I reached out and touched his cheek with my fingertip, absorbing one of his tears into my skin. Even though it felt like I was making contact with nothing but thin air, Dominic shivered a little. Like an electric connection had occurred between our souls.

He hit the brakes. The car slid sideways for a few feet, spraying mud and rocks. I thought the car was going to flip over. I braced myself, prepared for an impact or worse. We spun in a circle and the rotation moved us in the opposite direction of the tree.

Finally, the car came to a stop.

Dominic was breathing hard, gasping for air. He lowered his face against the steering wheel, overwhelmed by the moment. His entire body was shaking, wrought with adrenaline and fear. I fought the urge to hold him.

Soon enough. And then, forever.

His voice filled the space between us in the car. "I don't know who you are," he said. "But I know you're here with me."

"Yes, I am," I said. "And I always will be."

"You've always been here," he said. "Because you're my guardian angel."

"No," I said. "But I am your destiny."

CHAPTER TWELVE

There was a bright light shining in my eyes. It was blinding and disorienting. I squinted and blinked. I held my hand up and shielded my face.

Then I heard my Uncle Fred's voice. He was standing somewhere close to me. "Well, ladies and gentlemen. She might be my new assistant and she might only be fifteen, but she knows how to find her spotlight."

There were a few chuckles in the near distance.

Where am I?

I turned away from the light. I saw spots. I saw the red velvet curtain covered with gold and silver stars. I looked down. A black floor.

Help me. I'm onstage.

I turned back around to the audience. The spotlight was still so bright, I couldn't see their faces, but I knew they were there. I could sense them, hear them murmur and breathe.

"And now, for our final moment of the show…"

Uncle Fred took off his top hat, tapped the wide brim of it with his glittery-tipped wand, and out popped Carrots. There was a mild halfhearted applause.

My uncle handed Carrots to me. She squirmed and resisted and wriggled free. The audience started to howl with laughter. Carrots hopped around the stage a few times before scurrying off. I followed her. Still half-blinded from the stage lights, I tripped over her cage in the wings and tumbled to the floor. The audience laughed again. Even Sir Frederic the Great was having a tough time maintaining his composure. By the expression on his face, I couldn't tell if I was fired or if I was the most ridiculous thing he'd ever seen onstage at the Magic Mansion.

I captured Carrots and returned her safely to her cage. Then I stumbled my way into the claustrophobic dressing room.

Tasha and Topher were both there. They looked shell shocked. They were completely dazed.

Tasha was standing near the rack of old costumes wearing the black feathered boa around her shoulders. Topher was sitting on the checkered floor holding the Italian-English dictionary in his lap.

"What happened?" Topher asked. "Why are people laughing and cheering?"

"I just humiliated myself onstage," I said. "No big deal. I just have to change my name before school starts. Create a new identity."

"How did we get back here?" Tasha asked. "We were at Wonderland and—"

I lifted a finger and placed it against my lips. "Remember the rules," I said. "We can't talk about it. Not now. Not ever."

Tasha nodded. "You're right."

"We can't take any chances," I said. "Not after everything we just went through."

"But can I at least ask, did everything go as well as you wanted it to?" she said.

I nodded. "Yes," I said. "But I have no idea what happens next."

"None of us do," Topher added. "But he missed the plane."

"Yeah," Tasha said, "and she stayed onshore."

"Then just like Adrianna said…we wait…and we see," I said.

There was a knock right before the dressing room door opened. Tasha's face lit up at the sight of Sir Frederic the Great. "You don't want to take your bow?" he asked me.

"Um, what for?" I said. "So the audience can be reminded of how dreadful I was?"

"I have to be honest with you," he said.

"Please do."

"You were pretty dreadful."

"My feelings aren't hurt."

"Are you sure?" he asked. "Because I'd like to ask Tasha to be my new assistant."

Tasha let out a squeal. She leaped over to my uncle and gave him a big hug. "When do I start?"

"Tomorrow. At four o'clock. And don't be late."

Tasha tossed the boa around her neck and declared, "I wouldn't miss it for anything."

Clark suddenly appeared in the doorway. He stood next to my uncle. "Is this a private party in here?" he asked. "Or is the stage crew allowed to attend as well?"

"We're celebrating the end of my short-lived career as a magician's assistant," I said with a laugh. "It was over before it even started."

"Then in that case, we should probably order a pizza," Clark suggested.

"You read my mind," Uncle Fred told him.

"Yeah, I'm able to do that sometimes," Clark replied with a wink.

"Great. Over dinner I want to discuss some things," I said.

They all looked at me.

Did I say the wrong thing? Why is everyone staring?

"You sound so serious," Clark said. "Is everything okay?"

"No," I said. "The Magic Mansion is in deep trouble. And we all know it."

"Destiny, there's not much we can do about that," my uncle said. "Clark and I have tried everything. We can't force the bank to give us money. It doesn't work that way. We just don't have many more options."

I looked into my uncle's eyes. "Yes, we do," I said. "I've come up with some terrific ideas, some ways we can work together as a group to revitalize this place. We need to give it a new life. And fast."

"I like that," Clark said. "A new life."

"What sort of ideas do you have?" Uncle Fred asked.

"Well, for starters…we need to serve food," I said.

"Food?" they echoed.

"Clark will be in charge of creating a menu for the audience members. We can keep it simple but elegant. It will be easy enough to add some tables into the theater."

"Dinner and a magic show?" Clark said, smiling. "I like it."

"And don't forget dessert," I reminded him. "Also, Uncle Fred, you should start teaching classes."

"Me? A teacher?" he said. I could've sworn he was blushing.

"I want to create an apprentice program. A place where people can train to be magicians," I explained. "We desperately need to give the gift shop a makeover. We need to knock down a few walls. Expand. Put in a kitchen. We need a marquee outside. A real one. With lights. Also, we're going to start performing matinees. We can invite schools from all over South Carolina. Kids still love magic because they're not afraid to use their imaginations. And neither are we."

Everyone exchanged looks. Their eyes eventually shifted back to me.

They're staring at me like I'm an alien.

"Destiny, your ideas…they're fantastic," my uncle said. "Who knew you had such a great mind for business?"

I went to my uncle. We locked eyes, speaking silently. Without me saying a word, he knew I was accepting my legacy. I was embracing it. And even though I was only fifteen, I would do anything to make the Magic Mansion the success I knew it could be.

"You seem surprised," I said. "But it runs in my family."

❖

Days passed. Tasha, Topher, and I suffered from the restriction placed on us to never discuss what we'd experienced at Wonderland. This was even more difficult for me because I would never be allowed to share with my two best friends what happened in the final moments before I walked into Dominic's memory.

Once my decision was made, Adrianna had opened the door. I took a step forward into the darkness, but she stopped me by gently grabbing hold of my arm.

"You need to know something," she said. "Once you go through with this, you will never see me again. Not until you return to Wonderland someday."

"When will that be?" I asked.

"After you leave the world in which you now live."

I kissed my great-aunt's cheek, told her I loved her, and we said good-bye.

I walked into the wall of darkness. And I didn't look back.

Now the three of us were playing an awful waiting game.

It seemed we were each losing more hope with every day that went by without the reappearance of Dominic, Juliet, or Pablo. Little by little, I feared we were each giving up.

Renovations started almost immediately at the Magic Mansion. My uncle went back to the bank and revised his loan application. They only gave him half of the amount he asked for, but he felt certain it was enough to make some significant improvements.

Clark embraced his new role as a professional chef with an infectious lust for life. He spent most days trying out new recipes, all of which Tasha, Topher, and I were more than happy to sample.

School started and our lives were soon invaded by homework and the social politics of high school. I was the new girl and a bit of a novelty for the first few days. Soon, people got bored with the girl from Chicago who didn't have a Southern accent and lost interest in me altogether. This suited me just fine, as I was content with spending all of my free time with Tasha and Topher.

Boyd, Nathan, and Skeeter stopped chasing Topher. They'd moved on to tormenting a new kid who wore thick glasses and stuttered when he got nervous. I figured it was just a matter of time before someone turned the tables on the Neanderthals and gave them a taste of their own medicine. I even offered Boyd some words of advice when I saw him in the hallway at school. "Just remember," I said. "What goes around comes around."

❖

On a Wednesday, Tasha suggested the three of us meet up at the Irish coffeehouse after school. She even promised to treat me to a chocolate and banana smoothie, as if I needed any convincing to go. When I wasn't doing homework, I'd been spending every second at the Magic Mansion helping my uncles.

The three of us took over a table on the sidewalk, spreading out our textbooks. It was only the third week of school and I was already feeling behind. In fact, I was feeling disconnected from everything.

"I can't concentrate," I confessed. "All I think about is him."

My friends looked up from their homework and cell phones and offered me sympathetic looks.

Topher sighed. "I know exactly what you mean. It's making me crazy. I don't sleep much. I'm bored at school. I'm distracted by everything around me. I keep hoping…"

"I'm beyond the point of insanity," Tasha said. "I've even given up on comic books. Nothing can take my mind off her. If she doesn't show up soon, I'm dropping out of school and joining the Peace Corps."

Tasha stopped. Her eyes widened. Slowly, she stood up. She looked at me first and then at Topher. "Do you guys hear that?"

I listened. I shook my head. "Hear what? The ocean?"

"No," she said. "The music. Someone's playing a piano."

I listened again. "You're right," I agreed. "I hear it."

"Beethoven," she said.

Tasha glanced around, trying to figure out where the beautiful piano playing was coming from.

Moonlight Sonata.

Topher pointed up and across the street, to a shuttered window of a second-story apartment. "It's coming from up there."

Tasha wasted no time. She walked across the cobblestone

street and stood on the sidewalk below the window. She tilted her head back and shouted up to the second story, "Juliet!"

The piano stopped. Topher and I held our breath where we sat across the street. Seconds later, pale hands pushed open the red shutters covering the window's opening. Juliet appeared in the open window frame. She poked her head out and looked down to the street below. Her long auburn hair lifted in the delicate September afternoon breeze.

"It's about time, Tasha," she said, smiling. "What took you so long? Didn't someone tell you?"

"Tell me what?" Tasha said.

"You have to find us," Juliet explained. "We're not allowed to come and find you."

Topher and I exchanged a look before jumping out of our seats. We left everything behind and broke out into a run, heading toward the shoreline. It was six blocks to the playground. We didn't stop moving once.

All this time they've been waiting for us. They've been here all along. Adrianna, why didn't you tell us? Why make us suffer?

Topher and I were breathless and gasping for air when we stumbled into the huge pit of sand. The playground was empty. I saw disappointment flash across Topher's face.

"No one's here," Topher said. "I thought for sure..."

"Think, Topher. Where else could he be?" I asked.

Defeat crept into my friend's silvery blue eyes. "I hope he's not in Rome. Then what will I do?"

I shook my head. "No. He has to be here."

"But where?"

Topher's eyes drifted over to the cement tunnel. For so long the playground fixture had been his sanctuary, his necessary place of refuge. He moved across the playground in a hurry. He knelt down and peered inside his hideaway. The expression on Topher's face told me all I needed to know.

"Hello," Topher said. He reached inside the tunnel, offering his hand. Pablo emerged and stood up. He was just as handsome as I remembered him to be from the night we'd all danced in the courtyard at Wonderland.

"I was waiting for you," he explained. "You've been very busy, yes?"

Topher shook his head. For a second, I thought my friend was going to cry. "I'm just so happy," he said. "I'm even learning Italian for you."

Pablo smiled and wrapped his arms around Topher. "*Bellissimo*. I love you."

I felt awkward then. I knew I needed to leave and give them some privacy. "Topher, I'll meet you guys back at the café."

"Are you sure?" he asked. "We can wait for you."

"No," I said. "It's fine. I need to go somewhere first."

I walked away from Pablo and Topher. At first, I was going to embark on the six-block walk back to the café. There, I would finish my smoothie and hopefully get some homework done. Maybe later I'd meet up with Tasha and Juliet and Topher and Pablo. The five us could have pizza. Go see a movie. Maybe even stop by Bettina's and harass her for a while, just for fun.

Instead, I moved on instinct. Something told me not to go back to the café. For some reason I couldn't explain, I headed toward the ocean. I reached the top of a grassy hill and stared out at the sea. The majestic view was breathtaking. The water looked inviting and refreshing. Sailboats were drifting in different directions. The beach itself was populated by a few dozen people who were desperately clinging to the last days of summer. Girls in bikinis. Boys in swim trunks. Children building sandcastles. Couples riding by on rented bicycles, laughing and enjoying the gorgeous weather.

As I stood there looking down at the water's edge, I wondered if my mother had stood in the exact same spot.

Is this where you came up with your plan to leave Avalon Cove and never look back? Was it looking at this beach that made you want to see what else was out there, what the world had to offer you? Is this where you found the courage you needed to pursue your dreams?

I wondered if I would ever leave Avalon Cove. Even though I'd only lived there for a few weeks, it already felt like home. More and more, Chicago was becoming a distant memory. Already, it felt like another lifetime.

I made a mental note to call my brother. And also my father. I wanted them both to know I loved them, to tell them how much I had discovered about myself—about my family and where I came from—in just the short time I'd been in South Carolina. I also needed to call Samantha. Maybe I could convince her to come visit me during Christmas vacation. Or spend next summer with me in Avalon Cove. We had so much to catch up on.

I started to turn away from the water with plans to finally head back to the Irish café and order myself another chocolate and banana smoothie. I had homework to finish and more ideas to come up with on how to maximize the potential of the Magic Mansion.

Something caught my attention. I turned back to the sea.

Sitting farther down the beach was a male figure on a cobalt blue beach towel. He was hunched over a book of some kind. From where I was, I couldn't tell if he was drawing or reading. But it was clear he was captivated.

I moved out of curiosity, not quite sure if the man on the beach was Dominic. Yet, something was pulling me toward him. I kicked off my sandals and carried them. I welcomed the roughness of the warm sand against the skin between my toes. There was something comforting and soothing about the sensation.

Everything's going to be okay now. I can feel it. It's in the air.

I could hear the melody of the waves, lifting and rising and then spreading out across the sand, rolling in toward the island and the giggling children on the shore. Bits of conversations floated around me like the gentle whispers of ghosts. People were happy. They were relaxed. They were planning their futures together.

They were falling in love.

I reached the edge of his cobalt blue beach towel. His back was to me. I stared down at the top of his head. He was holding a sketch book in which he was drawing a picture of a girl. I took a closer look at the figure on the page.

It's me.

His hand froze. He sensed my presence. Slowly, he raised his face. He turned in my direction. Our eyes met. His mouth bloomed into a beautiful smile.

"I know you," he said.

I nodded. Emotions started to surge through me that were more powerful and intense than anything I'd ever felt before. "Yes," I said. "I think you do."

Dominic tossed his sketchbook aside. He stood up. We were face-to-face, eye to eye. "Correct me if I'm wrong," he said, "but I think you're my destiny."

I took a step closer, leaned in. I kissed him softly. The feeling of his lips against mine made me quiver. "That depends," I said, not able to take my eyes off him.

He slipped his hand into mine, pulled me closer, and grinned. "On what?" he asked.

I looked into his eyes. Then I turned and glanced out at the water and to the horizon beyond.

I took a deep breath and then asked the beautiful man standing beside me, "Do you believe in magic?"

About the Author

David-Matthew Barnes is the award-winning author of the novels *Mesmerized, Accidents Never Happen, Swimming to Chicago, The Jetsetters, Ambrosia,* and *Wonderland.* He is the writer and director of the films *Frozen Stars* and *Made From Scratch.* To date, he has written over forty stage plays that have been performed in three languages in eight countries. His literary work has been featured in over one hundred publications including *The Best Stage Scenes, The Best Men's Stage Monologues, The Best Women's Stage Monologues, The Comstock Review, Review Americana,* and *The Southeast Review.* David-Matthew was selected as the national winner of the 2011 Hart Crane Memorial Poetry Award. In addition, he has received the Carrie McCray Literary Award, the Slam Boston Award for Best Play, and earned double awards for poetry and playwriting in the World AIDS Day Writing Contest. He received a Master of Fine Arts in creative writing from Queens University of Charlotte in North Carolina. David-Matthew is a member of the Dramatists Guild of America and is on the faculty of the Spalding University brief-residency Master of Fine Arts in Writing Program.

Soliloquy Titles From Bold Strokes Books

Another 365 Days by KE Payne. Clemmie Atkins is back, and her life is more complicated than ever! Still madly in love with her girlfriend, Clemmie suddenly finds her life turned upside down with distractions, confessions, and the return of a familiar face... (978-1-60282-775-2)

The Secret of Othello by Sam Cameron. Florida teen detectives Steven and Denny risk their lives to search for a sunken NASA satellite—but under the waves, no one can hear you scream... (978-1-60282-742-4)

Andy Squared by Jennifer Lavoie. Andrew never thought anyone could come between him and his twin sister, Andrea...until Ryder rode into town. (978-1-60282-743-1)

Sara by Greg Herren. A mysterious and beautiful new student at Southern Heights High School stirs things up when students start dying. (978-1-60282-674-8)

Boys of Summer, edited by Steve Berman. Stories of young love and adventure, when the sky's ceiling is a sbright blue marvel, when another boy's laughter at the beach can distract from dull summer jobs. (978-1-60282-663-2)

Street Dreams by Tama Wise. Tyson Rua has more than his fair share of problems growing up in New Zealand—he's gay, he's falling in love, and he's run afoul of the local hip-hop crew leader just as he's trying to make it as a graffiti artist. (978-1-60282-650-2)

me@you.com by KE Payne. Is it possible to fall in love with someone you've never met? Imogen Summers thinks so because it's happened to her. (978-1-60282-592-5)

Swimming to Chicago by David-Matthew Barnes. As the lives of the adults around them unravel, high school students Alex and Robby form an unbreakable bond, vowing to do anything to stay together—even if it means leaving everything behind. (978-1-60282-572-7)

365 Days by KE Payne. Life sucks when you're seventeen years old and confused about your sexuality, and the girl of your dreams doesn't even know you exist. Then in walks sexy new emo girl, Hannah Harrison. Clemmie Atkins has exactly 365 days to discover herself, and she's going to have a blast doing it! (978-1-60282-540-6)

Cursebusters! by Julie Smith. Budding psychic Reeno is the most accomplished teenage burglar in California, but one tiny screw-up and poof!—she's sentenced to Bad Girl School. And that isn't even her worst problem. Her sister Haley's dying of an illness no one can diagnose, and now she can't even help. (978-1-60282-559-8)

Who I Am by M.L. Rice. Devin Kelly's senior year is a disaster. She's in a new school in a new town, and the school bully is making her life miserable—but then she meets his sister Melanie and realizes her feelings for her are more than platonic. (978-1-60282-231-3)

Sleeping Angel by Greg Herren. Eric Matthews survives a terrible car accident only to find out everyone in town thinks he's a murderer—and he has to clear his name even though he has no memories of what happened. (978-1-60282-214-6)

Mesmerized by David-Matthew Barnes. Through her close friendship with Brodie and Lance, Serena Albright learns about the many forms of love and finds comfort for the grief and guilt she feels over the brutal death of her older brother, the victim of a hate crime. (978-1-60282-191-0)